ALWAYS A

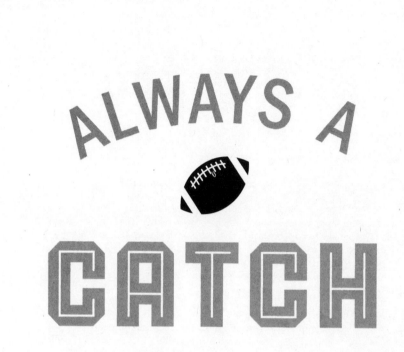

ALWAYS A CATCH

PETER RICHMOND

Philomel Books, an Imprint of Penguin Group (USA)

PHILOMEL BOOKS
Published by the Penguin Group
Penguin Group (USA) LLC
375 Hudson Street, New York, NY 10014

USA | Canada | UK | Ireland | Australia | New Zealand | India | South Africa | China
penguin.com
A Penguin Random House Company

Library of Congress Cataloging-in-Publication Data is available upon request.
Library of Congress Cataloging-in-Publication Data
Richmond, Peter, 1953–
Always a catch / Peter Richmond.
pages cm
Summary: After he joins the new football team, Jack, a new junior and a skilled
piano player at a preparatory boarding school, must decide how far he is willing
to go to fit in with his new teammates, and how much he is willing to compromise
himself to play the kind of music the school expects him to.
[1. Boarding schools—Fiction. 2. Schools—Fiction. 3. Pianists—Fiction.
4. Self-realization—Fiction. 5. Football—Fiction.] I. Title.
PZ7.R4144Al 2014
[Fic]—dc23
2013045424

Printed in the United States of America.
ISBN 978-0-399-25055-2
1 3 5 7 9 10 8 6 4 2

Edited by Jill Santopolo. Design by Siobhán Gallagher.
Text set in 11.25-point ITC New Baskerville Std.

For Burr Johnson and his family

1

"HERE IT IS!" I COULD HEAR my dad shouting down the crazy long hallway in our apartment. The floor's made of marble and everything echoes, especially the sound of his fancy shoes now coming down to my room. He barged right in, just as I was dropping my hoplites out of their siege tower on top of the Trojans' wall.

"Thanks for knocking," I said.

He was holding a fat envelope. He hadn't even loosened his tie. "This is from Oakhurst Hall, Jack!"

"So?" I said.

"So the envelope is thick! That means you're in! Here, open it!"

By now my guys were getting hacked to pieces and I was going to lose the battle in *Odysseus's Revenge* anyway. So I took it. I hadn't really thought about what would happen if had to make the Decision. I never thought I had a chance in hell of getting in to Oakhurst Hall.

I pulled out a pile of forms on pink and yellow paper, with one white one, written on thick stationery topped by

Oakhurst Hall's crest. It had a lion on it. "Dear Jack," it said, "It gives us great pleasure . . ."

"And?" said his father.

"I'm in," I said. "Here." I gave him back all the papers.

"Well, you don't sound very excited for a boy who's just been accepted in to one of the best schools in the world."

"That's because I'm not," I said. "Excited, I mean." Which was true. Mostly I was confused.

Dad was obviously trying not to explode. "Don't you have any ambition at all?"

This was a conversation we had about twice a week. Correction: make that five times a week.

"I didn't know I was supposed to know what I wanted to do already," I said, as usual.

"Well," he said, "I did when I was your age." As usual.

"No, you were just ashamed that granddad had a fishing boat on the Cape, so you had to reinvent yourself. And you did. Way to go."

The whole thing had been his idea. One night, after he'd already had about four glasses of wine because his company had closed a deal to build a hockey arena in Canada somewhere—that's his job—he told me I was going to apply to transfer to some prep school in the woods for eleventh grade.

"Fine," said Dad. "Play video games for the rest of your life. Turn your back on a great opportunity."

I started the game over.

"And speaking of opportunities," he said, right before he slammed the door, "maybe you'd better give this a little more thought. I can change my will with a ten-second call to my lawyer."

His steps echoed back down the hallway, even faster this time.

Did he really just say that?

Did I care?

I texted my best friend, Luke:

Yo. Prepworld wants me. Haven't decided. If I don't go, my dad says I won't inherit his money . . . as if I care. OK, yeah, maybe I do.

Thirty seconds passed. Then Luke answered:

May Satan have mercy on your soul.

Nobody spoke a word until dessert, when Grace said, "Does everyone like the sea-salt caramel gelato?"

Dad didn't say anything. So I said, "Okay, I'll go."

What I didn't say was that Dad had made the decision for me. It was time to get away from this place.

"That's *great*, Jack," he said, trying not to jump up and high-five himself because now he could tell the next cocktail party he had a kid at Oakhurst Hall, founded fifty centuries ago.

"Oh, sweetie, that's such good news," said Grace.

"This calls for a toast." Dad pulled a bottle of '92 Château Margaux and the crystal glasses out of the cabinet. He opened the bottle slowly, like he was operating on a baby or something. God forbid the cork should break. Then he raised his glass. "To becoming a man."

I took a sip of the wine, and then another. Okay, it was good. My dad and Grace let me drink wine at home because apparently that's what they do in Europe. I wasn't complaining.

"Jack," Dad said, "you're doing the right thing."

"I know I am," I heard myself say. And maybe for once I *was* doing the right thing.

DAD WAS SAYING SOMETHING TO ME from the front seat. I couldn't hear him, because I had my headphones on, but I already knew it was something like, "You'll make contacts that will last you the rest of your life, Jack," which was something he'd said about eleven times since I'd gotten in to Oakhurst Hall.

I took the headphones off. The electro chords of Glitch Mob gave way to the sound of Dad's lecture voice.

"... *presidents.*"

"Presidents what?" I said.

"*Two* presidents attended Oakhurst Hall, Jack. *Two.*"

Great. No pressure. "So you'll be disappointed if I don't become president?"

"Jack, sarcasm isn't necessary," Grace said. Grace wasn't really that bad. She was sort of a fake, my stepmother, but you kind of had to like her because she tried so hard to be what she wasn't. She was from a family in Jersey that sold tires until she got a job with my dad's company. His job is to get the land to build these stadiums, even if there are people already living there in houses. He finds ways to force them to move. I wasn't sure it was the kind of thing I'd want to get paid for. Not that I had a clue in that department.

I *did* know for sure, as he always reminded me, that he'd had to work eleven jobs or something to pay for the business-school degree after he went to Colgate on a hockey scholarship. This was something else he also liked to talk about a lot: his hockey days in college, when he had "limited talent" but "made the most of it." Which I figured meant that he was the guy who did the fighting. The funny thing was, even with his Zegna suits and perfect haircuts, his nose still gave him away—broken a couple of times, a little off center, with a little bump halfway up. I think it helped him close deals: a guy's guy who'd learned how to play with the big boys.

"The point is," he was saying, over his shoulder, "we're doing this for you. We want you to have all the best opportunities possible."

"You mean so I can get the opportunity to buy a bottle of wine that costs what someone in Ghana makes in a year?"

I wasn't always that snarky, but sometimes the stuff he said was just too easy a target.

The real point of all of this was that, without knowing it, he'd given me a chance to get out of New York City and figure out some way for life to not be so boring.

"No, to be *happy*," he said. "Happiness and success go hand in hand."

Another piece of wisdom from your friends at www. fortunecookie.com.

I hit the window button so I didn't have to smell Grace's perfume anymore. My own mom didn't wear perfume—I didn't think. It had been a while. Which probably explained a lot. About me, I mean.

She'd been living somewhere in Guatemala in a clay hut for the least eight years, teaching kids how to play the flute and love Jesus Christ. I guess if I'd been married to Dad, I'd have gone to a jungle, too. I didn't actually blame her. At least, I didn't on the day she decided she had "good work" to do a couple thousand miles away, because when you're eight years old, you don't really think about the work she hasn't finished doing with you yet. She's your mom. You trust her.

So Grace did her best, and time passed, but what didn't stop sucking was that if one day your mother was there and the next day she wasn't, well, you sort of started asking yourself, *Who* else *is going to walk away for good?* I figured if I backed away first, or put up some sort of video-game force field, then I was the one doing the leaving.

"I'll settle for you being president of your class," Dad said, with half a laugh—half because I knew he actually meant it. "But I doubt that Oakhurst Hall chooses its class leaders because they won the tenth-grade music prize. You better play the hell out of that piano. Since sports isn't exactly your strong suit."

That again. As if I'd ever had a chance on the Upper West Side of Manhattan? When the baseball field is caged in on the roof?

Nice vote of confidence.

"So if you don't even think I'm gonna make it at this place," I said, "why are we doing this?"

"Jack, I think you'll do just great," he said, "and finding the right friends is going to help. Remember, sometimes to make the right friends, you have to reach out more than halfway."

This, of course, was about how I didn't have any real friends other than Luke at home, which had to mean there was something wrong with me. The psychologist back at the U—"the University School"—as if—did some tests after a couple of teachers said I was "guarded" and "cautious." One teacher said I was "dark," which was pretty ridiculous, considering when I wasn't in school I liked to mostly go to jam band concerts where everyone was grinning like a madman from the contact high and I ended up dancing with random girls and getting a contact madman grin of my own.

So the psychologist prescribed me three different drugs in one year. One made me puke, one made me feel like I was wearing a suit of armor, and the third kept me up all night with the same Zeppelin loop going around in my head. I stopped taking everything and started running around the Reservoir, which always turned in to the best high you can get.

"So," I said, "I have to make the right friends so they can make me a success?"

"No," he said. "I've always told you there's only one way to the top: try harder than the people on each side of you, until you're the only one at the top. Survival of the fittest."

And, yeah, he always had said that, about once every six months. Me, I saw the point in trying hard. But harder? So I could be, what? Basically, thanks to music, at least I was afloat, although music wasn't exactly something you made a living at, and if you did, it'd probably ruin the fun anyway.

Maybe here, three hundred miles away from Dad and my fake classmates like Ty, who was a die-hard Knicks fan—because his family had courtside season tickets—and Diggy, who liked to listen to hop-hop while he was on the beach in the Hamptons, in a place with some new girls I could find something else I was good at. Something that other people couldn't ruin.

WHEN WE FINALLY GOT TO NEW HAMPSHIRE, it was dark and rainy. We drove up the long Oakhurst Hall driveway past a rusty, curved iron wall standing in the middle of a field. "That is a *terrific* Serra," my dad said. This meant that the wall was made by a famous artist, although I thought it looked like part of a building that had fallen down.

The cars in the lot next to St. John Hall, the main castle of the place, looked like big silver and black beetles. A couple of limos in front of the big wooden doors were too cool for parking. A soaking-wet blue and gold Oakhurst Hall banner stretched over the entrance, roped at each end to weird lion gargoyles that were laughing and snarling at the same time, like they were in on a joke no one else got. A bell somewhere droned one deep note, again and again.

Very cheery.

The walls of the dining room had a lot of oil portraits of old headmasters who all had dogs next to them. None of the people or the dogs were smiling. I stood in this long line for registration. My parents had been sent somewhere to listen to the dean explain the school rules.

I was nervous, probably because I still wasn't sure why they'd taken me. I mean, there had to be better piano players. My best guess was that Dad had told them he'd donate a mil toward a second hockey rink or something.

It sure wasn't my interview last spring, with a guy wearing a yellow tie with blue lacrosse sticks on it. His name was Mr. McGregor, but he said I could call him Phil. I didn't. He was sitting in a blue leather wing-backed chair, and his teeth were too white. A pile of files was stacked on his desk. Out the window, kids were playing touch football down on a quad bordered by an old iron fence painted black. I wanted to be in that game. The fireplace crackled, though, and I liked that part.

When Phil asked me what my hobbies were, all I could come up with was "running around the Reservoir in Central Park." This was kind of true, because after school, when home wasn't where I wanted to be, I'd run around the Reservoir and try to pass everyone, until I couldn't run anymore and it was dark and you could see the lights of the buildings on all sides of the park like jewels.

My dad never believed me when I showed up sweating after dark and said I'd been running. But then, I never believed him when he said that all the families his company shoved out of their neighborhoods were "fairly compensated." There wasn't a lot we agreed on.

I hadn't wanted to tell McGregor that I played the piano,

because saying the piano was a hobby wasn't fair to my piano. It was more than a hobby. The real reason I liked it was that when I was playing the piano, I wasn't thinking. Just feeling. Or trying to find the right song to make me feel the right way. Which I thought was sort of what Zen Buddhism was supposed to be, only with a soundtrack.

But I could tell Phil was getting bored, so I said, "I play the piano pretty well, too." This seemed to wake him up a little.

"Want to know something funny?" he asked. In my experience, that means that whatever someone is about to say isn't funny. "I had a band at St. Lawrence. Lead guitar! We covered Lynyrd Skynyrd. Hard to believe, huh?"

Well, hard to believe anyone would want to cover Skynyrd, yeah. Then I lied about being on the squash ladder, and McGregor said something like, "Business is conducted on the golf course, but the *real* important decisions are made on the squash court."

The rest of my file was probably teachers saying "Jack is still finding himself." As if anyone had ever told me where to look.

But maybe this place would be a good place to start, I had thought, when I left McGregor's office, because this girl with long brown hair wearing gray everything except for a pearl necklace, waiting to go in next, gave me a shy smile and looked away.

She had *so* definitely looked. This didn't happen a lot. Back at the U, girls sort of looked through me. I didn't think I was bad looking, but I didn't have any of those sharp angles people talked about, like cheekbones on models or the noses on Roman statues.

It's hard to describe what I look like, because I don't look like anything. I could be a police artist's composite sketch of the kid everyone is trying to find, only there's no chance in hell of finding him, because in the picture there's fuzziness all over the edges and details. No *there* there.

Maybe here, though, there'd *be* something there. Like that girl in gray.

"HELLO, JACK. WE'RE SO EXCITED TO see you!" The woman behind the table held out a folder with my name on it.

JACK LEFFERTS.

She was wearing a pink sweater with a gold leaf pin up
near her shoulder blade. She had hair that was sort of like a
TV weather lady. "You're in Scoville House," she said. "And
you'll be seeing a lot of me! I'm Ginny Ward! Tom and I are
your dorm parents!"

Dorm parents? I already had more than enough parents.

"Your roommate is Josh McPhail. This is his third year,
so he'll be able to get you up to speed. Tonight at dinner,
you'll be sitting at Mr. Carlton's headmaster table with some
of the other new fifth formers, and you can tell him all about
yourself!"

That'd take about eleven seconds.

At the music registration table, a thin girl with brown
hair who smelled really good was telling some old guy with
slicked white hair and wire-rimmed glasses that she played
the flute. When she walked away, it was her—the girl in gray.
Yes!

The man stuck out his hand. "Jack, I'm Mr. Hopper! I hear you're a Tchaikovsky guy!" he said.

"Well, I haven't done much practicing this summer," I said. This was true. About the Tchaikovsky, anyway. I'd done a lot of playing, but just trying to write songs, and I didn't think this guy was into his students writing indie songs.

"I hope not! Summer is for relaxing," said Hopper. "Now we get down to business! We'll be meeting once a week for your private lesson. As you know, the top pianist in the fall term competition gets to play with the symphony at the Thanksgiving concert. Over the years, I don't mind telling you, the labels have sent *quite a few scouts.*"

Scouts?

"And his year's concert has drawn some television interest. Of course, whether Mr. Carlton will allow cameras into our family's biggest night of the year is something I can't predict. But that's all the more reason to study those sonatas, isn't it? Have you ever played a Steinway built in 1859, Jack? On that evening, the student who's won First Piano will. Think about *that,* Jack."

I didn't really want to.

The line at the sports sign-up table was long, which gave me time to reconsider the possibly stupid thing I was about to do.

At University, I did rec-everything. In the fall, it was soccer, which didn't feel like a sport because a half hour could go by without me kicking the ball, even though the coach kept saying, "Jack, you *know* you're a natural athlete. Why don't you get more involved in the flow of the game?" Well, first off, because I didn't want to get kicked in the shins by some maniac from some other rival school. I didn't mind getting hit playing a sport. I just minded rich kids playing a game like assholes.

In the winter, it was squash, which I was also apparently pretty good at, except everyone acted like someone from an Abercrombie catalogue, so I played club. In the spring, they kept telling me to run track, because I was really fast, but I didn't like track because there was no *team*. Wasn't sports supposed to be about *teams*?

At home, in the apartment, the only sport Dad and I watched was Yankees games, which didn't exactly help the relationship. Dad liked them. I hated them because they bought all the best players, and Kansas City couldn't afford to pay anyone anything.

"Real fans don't root for the team," Dad said. "They root for the uniform." Which was like saying you had to like invading Afghanistan because the army uniforms were the same ones they wore in World War II.

But twice each fall, Luke took me out to a Giants game, which was completely cool, like a real video game, like when the Greeks decided to play sports instead of actually killing each other. It was even fun getting inside the stadium.

In the parking lot, everyone was smashed and grilling meat and throwing footballs, and for the hell of it Luke and I would always just stop and join in someone's game, tossing the ball. It became a tradition with us. In those catches, with fans from Jersey and kids from Brooklyn, footballs seemed to like my hands, maybe because my fingers were so long. I was terrible at throwing them, but since I'd never played the game—University didn't have a team because the parents didn't want their kids to get hurt—those random games of catch out in the Giants' stadium parking lot were a really cool detour from the rest of my life.

And then, when the Giants scored a touchdown, this huge stadium actually shook, which was scary in a good way: 80,000 drunken people could make cement and steel move because *someone had caught a football.* And all the players had helmets on, which meant that the game wasn't about who was handsome and who wasn't, or who was ripped and who was fat, or even who was black and who was white (at least from the top of the upper deck, where Luke's seats were).

One thing I knew for sure: when I had played piano at the U's "Evening of Musical Magic" last year, I *nailed* the stupid Mozart, but when I finished, no one was standing up sloshing his beer in a plastic cup and high-fiving the guy next to him. And that was supposedly the highlight of my budding musical career.

. . .

The guy behind the athletic table was sort of shaped like a muscular cube. His tie was really loud. "I'm the AD," he said, pumping my hand without looking at me. "I see you're a soccer guy. Terrific. We've got a JV team, and the thirds are pretty competitive."

"I kind of changed my mind," I said. "I'm going out for football."

He looked up at me as if I'd said something in Mandarin. "Well, okay," he said. "Good. Sure, Whatever. So JV tryouts are tomorrow, three o'clock. That's if you want to, you know, stay with that choice. Football."

"Yeah," I said. "I do." Why not? What could happen? Other than I break some bones? Besides, girls are supposed to be into football players.

"Okay, then." The guy flicked a checkmark onto his clipboard, then looked over my shoulder, and grinned. "Zowitzki! Dude!"

I turned around. A kid was staring at me with crazy-bright blue eyes. He had a blond buzz cut, and acne sprinkled his face like measles. His shoulders were about twice as wide as his waist. He was hopping from one foot to the other, as if he was listening to music. But he didn't have any headphones on.

"We missed you in camp, Swicky," the AD said.

"Yeah, well, summer school just ended yesterday," the

Zowitzki kid answered. "I aced that math shit. And I'm ready."

"Tell me something I don't know. We all are. This is the year."

I drifted away.

The dorm room was in an old, dark building with heavy wooden doors. The first floor had a large lounge, a flat-screen on the wall, and some couches. My room, on the fourth floor, was small, but the view was pretty cool: trees and soccer fields, leading to the foot of a small mountain on the south side of the campus.

It looked as if my roommate had already checked in. A pile of textbooks lay on the top bunk, which had already been made. An open MacBook Air sat on one of the desks next to a pile of CDs: Feist, Elbow, the Decemberists, all pretty emo. His screen saver was the girl from the *Dragon Tattoo* movie. Two guitars leaned against a wall, and lots of magazines covered the floor: *Mojo, INDIE, Spin, Guitar Player.*

Grace put my clothes in the empty dresser and hung my jackets in the closet, and for a second or two, she seemed like a mom.

My father looked through one of my roommate's econ textbooks. "Impressive," he said. "There's a whole chapter on low-end derivatives. Looks like we might just get our money's worth."

· · ·

In the parking lot, Grace hugged me. "It's going to be *fabulous*. I know you'll love it. But keep your nose clean! That dean was a little . . . *strict* . . . wasn't he, honey? And what about that girl who almost died?"

"Well, it was pretty routine, I thought, for a place like this," Dad said.

A place like this? That sounded a little ominous.

"Your dorm parent owns your cell phone," he said. "If you're not doing approved research, the internet is open two hours at night, twice a week, and if you try to hack your way in, they'll hack you out of school."

"Tell him the . . . the hospital part," Grace prodded him.

"Well, yeah. He said they're real strict on the drinking and drug thing now, because they had to boot two kids last spring for making moonshine in the chem lab and then nearly killing themselves with it. One of them had to be hooked up to a respirator for a week. Pretty industrious, though."

He tried to say it loosely, but I could see a slant of worry in Grace's eyes.

"Now, if you get homesick," she said, "just e-mail us when you're allowed to."

"Well, he won't be homesick," said Dad. "He had no problem being away for a month on Outward Bound last summer."

That was another one of Dad's character-building ideas,

filed under "trying to make you what you're not"—although since I didn't know who I *was*, I had to cut him some slack. The funny thing was, I liked it. On my solo trip, the desert felt like Mars. Plus, with all the rock climbing, I put on some muscles—not muscles that you could see, but I could feel them anyway. Coming home on the plane, I imagined I had a superpower that no one could see. Okay, maybe just a power.

Dad clicked his keys to unlock the car. Like someone was going to steal it at a prep school.

"I'll keep you posted on football," I said.

His hand stopped as he was opening the door. "Going out for football?"

"Yeah, well, why not? I thought I'd try it."

"Aren't you a little light to be playing football?" he said, pretending to joke, but not pulling it off.

"Don't worry," I said. "I'll dull the pain with moonshine."

Dad's goodbye handshake was like a fish fillet. The Lexus disappeared down the drive with the tires squishing. The rain was picking up.

I walked back toward the quad with the old iron railings. There was a touch football game going on, like last spring when I was interviewing with McGregor. One of the kids threw a long, wild pass, way out of bounds—right at me, but over my head. I threw my hands up, and suddenly, it was as if the ball was slowing down, like those old slow-motion films they show of games back in the Dark Ages with all that heavy

Russian classical *DUM-dada-DUM* music, like the games were artillery battles on some battlefield in the Balkans.

Then, I swear, I don't know why, but I could see the rotation of the ball and the writing on the label—SPALDING—and even the little dimples on the leather. This wasn't like the parking lot outside the Giants' stadium. This time, for some reason, part of my brain had decided to get super-focused. And somehow the ball rolled perfectly into my palms. It curled to a stop. I felt like it belonged to my fingers.

I underhanded the ball to a kid on the other side of the fence.

"Nice catch," he said. "Good hands."

Good hands. That sounded nice.

I started walking away, but I had to stop because I didn't have a clue how to get back to my dorm.

"You lost?" It was a tall guy with skin like an iced-coffee with two shots of half and half, a medium Afro, and a goatee.

I shrugged. "Uh, maybe."

"What form?"

"Fifth," I said.

"They probably stuck you in Screwville. Big old gloomy building? Back-ass end of the campus?"

"That sounds right," I said.

"Follow that path over there, take a left at the equestrian statue." He could tell I didn't know what he was talking about and smiled. "Horse statue. It's an old dude on a horse, with a sword. I think he defended Oakhurst Hall in the Revolutionary War." The guy loped off into the rain, then turned back. "Guillermo Martin. They call me Will."

"Jack Lefferts."

He flashed a peace sign and was gone.

I found the statue, found the gloomy hall, and climbed the stairs. Pieces of different kinds of music filtered out from each hallway, some Talking Heads, some Foos. I made it to the fourth floor without even breathing that hard. Outward Bound and the Reservoir. I was in shape.

"You're a piano player, right?" was the first thing the kid on the top bunk in our room said. He had a shaved head a few days later than he'd shaved it, and he was wearing a sleeveless Killers T-shirt. He was wired. "What kind of music you into? New Garage? Electroclash? Punk DIY? We have a band. We could really use a keyboard. We're indie all the way, like, Elbow meets King Crimson. A little Pixies, some Yeah Yeah Yeahs, and this year it's time for a major dose of TV on the Radio. Not that I wouldn't rule out a little Phish."

"You're talking my language," I said. "Jams rule."

He nodded like I'd passed some kind of first test. "And we need a drummer too, since Chipper got booted. He was too Allmans anyway. Word is this new Simon kid plays pretty good, but that he's sort of a freakazoid." Then he hopped down from the bunk and shook my hand. "Josh."

"Jack," I said. It was a good handshake. Like, whatever the handshake was invented for, he had it down. "So what'd your roommate do?" I said.

He vaulted back up onto his bunk and reached for a copy of *Vice* that had a girl with a tattooed forehead standing in front of a power plant. With the internet shut off most of the time I guessed that Oakies had to actually read paper magazines. It was like being in a place back in another time.

"Illegal cell phone with five speed-dial porn lines," he said, "and twenty-five demerits in one year: the world record. First time someone had ever said 'fuck you' to Chipper Pratt."

"So what happened to him?" I asked. I wanted to find out what the boundaries were in this place and what happened if you went outside them. I already knew that I was going to stretch them.

"He's in one of those 'therapeutic' schools," Josh said, "where they have wards instead of forms."

This was a word I still hadn't grokked. "What's the deal with 'forms,' anyway?"

"It has something to do with old military formations," Josh said, now leafing through *High Times*. I was guessing he didn't get it through an Oakhurst Hall mail-room subscription. "We're here for old Oak to form us." He barked a one-syllable laugh. "Good luck on that. My dad went here. His dad went here. They both won the Brightfield Prize. I'll be breaking that tradition. Or, make that 'shattering.'"

"So, what, you didn't want to go here?" I said.

"I wanted to go to Putney and carry milk pails," he said. "Instead I had to carry on the tradition. When I got in here two years ago, I asked McGregor why in hell they accepted me. I mean, the family name was big here in the Middle Ages, but the money is, like, gone. My great-great-grandfather invented something called 'men's hair tonic.' McGregor told me that my aptitude evaluations said I was way advanced in science things. So I guess I had to come here to get into Caltech and design missiles and leave a trillion to the old Hall. All I knew was that I wanted out. From home. Lake Forest, Illinois. And think about *that*: How can you have a lake and a forest at the same time?"

"Yeah," I said. "My world was kind of fake too. But I try not think about it much."

"So you got in for the piano? Or you do a sport?"

"I'm going out for JV football," I said.

Josh dropped the magazine into his lap and looked me in the eye. "Seriously? You don't look like a meathead. You some sort of football prodigy?"

"I don't know," I said. "No, I mean. No. I never played."

Josh laughed loud, shaking his head. "Watch your ass. The football boys are kind of, like, territorial. They think they're the fucking royalty or something, which our esteemed headmaster Carlton thinks they are too."

Turned out that when Carlton played quarterback for

Notre Dame, someone broke his leg with a dirty hit. He coached for a while in western Pennsylvania. Then he hit the prep hamster wheel at some middle school in Massachusetts. Wife left him when he had an affair with somebody in the development office, and he got this gig. Then two years ago, Josh told me, we'd won our league, but they took the cup away when somebody found out that one of the coaches had been filming upcoming opponents. Carlton was on a mission to win it legit.

"I'll probably be thirds," I said. "I don't want to take it serious or anything."

"Son, it's all serious around here with sports," Josh said. "Wait'll you hear Carlton's sermon about how the British Empire started on the playing fields of some fancy prep school back in the twelfth century or something. As far as I can tell, they all buggered each other, then married their cousins. Some empire." He went back to *High Times,* and said, "So, Jack Lefferts, you like to get *nice?*"

The truth was, I did get high, if someone else was smoking, but only like the way I'd drink beer at one of the bars on the Upper East Side that served preppies if I was with Luke or one of the girls I asked out, but somehow never hooked up with. Mostly I didn't like the way weed made me feel dumber.

"Yeah, sometimes," I said. "You?"

"Usually practice nights for the band, after dinner, back

of the arts building—if we have a band this year. And if we can get you and this Simon kid together with me and Danny, we could actually *have* a band. The practice room we use, you take a right at the end of the Hall of Piano Champions—you can't miss the trophies—until you see the room that looks like a closet. There's an old upright. Probably kind of out of tune. But I don't think the Stasi faculty drones even know the room is there."

"So that's where you get high? Or where you jam?"

"Well, both. But we can definitely smoke. Scoville's where we gotta be careful. Ward is gonna be CSI Oakhurst Hall this year. Last year, he busted three rooms in one night—vodka, pot, porn. The trifecta. The weed guy got booted. The vodka guy had to clean out the sports buses for a week, which means scrubbing scummy rubber floor mats with a rag, since half of them dip. But if it's a girl's team, you might come across some items that are highly sellable in the football dorm."

The door suddenly swung open—no knock—revealing the entire Ward family: a life-sized snapshot of the American dream. Mr. Ward was about thirty, with a receding hairline and a frown. My guess was that Josh wasn't his favorite dorm kid. His wife was in a dress full of flowers, and her face had that same frozen smile I first saw at registration. Two small blond children stood behind them: a girl of about five in a flowered dress like her mom's and a boy about four in denim overalls that looked pressed and dry-cleaned.

"Hi, Jack!" Mrs. Ward said. "This is Tom, your dorm floor master, and this is Jess and Tommy."

Tom Ward stepped forward and offered and a man-to-man nod and handshake, way too hard, but he was looking straight at Josh. "The hair grows back, McPhail. Starting yesterday."

"Last year you said it was too long, Mr. Ward," said Josh. "I only—"

"Hi, guys," I said to the little kids, who immediately ran behind their mother.

"We're just on our way to dinner," said the wife. "Jack, we wanted to welcome you to the fourth floor of Scoville."

"McPhail, you already know the drill," Ward said to Josh. "So, Lefferts, lights-out is eleven. No exceptions. The internet is turned on for two hours, nine to eleven, two nights a week. No one knows the days in advance. Rest of the time, dark. Cell phones belong to me." He paused. "Lefferts: your phone." I reached into my pocket and hit the Off button, then handed him, basically, my old life. Other than Luke, I didn't really think I'd miss it. "Wake-up is six forty-five, breakfast is seven thirty."

Now Ward swung an imaginary golf club, driving an imaginary golf ball down some imaginary fairway in some imaginary country club, and then, just as quick, he was back on earth. "If you fail three room inspections in a week," he said, putting my phone in his khaki pocket, "no dorm lounge privileges for the following week. Also, no food in the room. No loud music. Especially no rap."

No rap? What kind of rule was that?

"No problem there," I said. "Never touch the stuff." For a second, I thought I'd crossed the line. But no one had been listening to me anyway.

"Hip-hop—can't stand it," said Ward, mostly to himself. "And one more thing: rooms are always open to search."

He turned and walked out, followed by his wife and their ducklings. Then the door suddenly opened again. Mrs. Ward stuck her face in, with her cardboard smile. "You really don't want to be late to dinner, dear," she said to me, ignoring Josh. "Remember, this is your first week, and you can only make a first impression once."

Then she was gone again.

I had to tell my dad about that one. It was such a Dad saying.

Yeah, they were definitely another set of parents. Great.

RIGHT BEHIND CARLTON'S TABLE, TWO LARGE bronze lion heads topped the andirons in the fireplace, which was big enough to walk into. This was obviously Table Number One.

The good news: the girl in gray from McGregor's office last spring was standing to my right.

The bad news: the entire place was as freaking silent as a church. Everyone was waiting for Carlton to say the year's first grace. It turned out to be something about the Lord and nourished souls. Then a senior table proctor in a madras jacket and a monogrammed shirt rushed off to get our food. A couple of guys in blue fleece sweatshirts with OAKHURST HALL MAINTENANCE emblems showed up out of nowhere to throw some logs on the fire, then disappeared just as quickly.

"Welcome, people!" said Carlton to all us new eleventh graders. "We've had great luck with our entering fifth formers in the last few years. But I'll bet you're going to outshine them all!"

He was trying so hard to be a headmaster it was like he was auditioning for that Robin Williams movie about a prep-school teacher. Or maybe it was all an act. Maybe he was actually supposed to have been the quarterback of Luke's Giants—only everything went different, and someone forced him into this alternate universe.

"So how about we all introduce ourselves, give a little thumbnail sketch?" he said, with the fake grin. "I'm Charles Carlton: Fay '77, Groton '81, Notre Dame '85, Columbia '87. Hobbies: books, backgammon, and being sure to learn something new every day."

A fat kid on my left named Spencer said his hobby was string theory. I wasn't paying attention; I was trying to pick up the soft scent of the shampoo to my right without being too obvious. I heard Carlton say my name.

"I'm from New York," I said. "I like playing the piano."

"Your name precedes you, Mr. Lefferts," he said. "You're fortunate to be working with Mr. Hopper. He's quite the star in our firmament."

"And," I said, "I'm going out for football."

"Well, you'll find our JVs are very competitive," Carlton said. For the first time, his central-casting expression changed into something like confusion, since, I guess, none of the advance intelligence he'd gotten included me and the football thing. So he quickly asked about the girl with the good hair.

"I'm Caroline Callahan," she said shyly, carefully laying her silverware on her plate. "I play the flute, and I run cross-country." Then she looked at me, and I almost got excited, until I figured she was probably doing it because we both did music, and she didn't want to be impolite by staring at her plate anymore.

The kid to Caroline's right spoke next. I liked him immediately. His eyes were nearly totally hidden by his bangs. "I'm Simon Ridgway. I was born up in Boston, on a hill that's supposed to be famous. Now I live in Brooklyn, on another hill."

"Beacon," said Carlton, "and Cobble. Am I right?"

"That's them," said Simon. I could tell that the Simon kid was fucking around with Carlton. "I play all the classics: *Doom, Surreal,* and *Grand Theft Auto—San Andreas.*"

Carlton obviously didn't know what the kid was talking about. "And didn't your father get a MacArthur Fellowship just a few years ago?"

"Yeah. The 'genius' award. As *if.*"

"Well, as I understand it, you're the latest in a long line of quite brilliant scholars," Carlton said, without listening to the kid. "And you were the winner of a statewide Latin competition last year."

"Yeah," he said. "But I'm dropping Latin up here."

"Really." Carlton was no longer smiling. "Do tell us why."

"Because," the kid answered, weighing each word like an actor onstage, "*it has ensnared me in the cold, dead grip of tradition.*"

"Excuse me?" said Carlton.

"That's from a graphic novel about turning zombies back into humans through microbial reanimation."

Then the rest of the table recited their lives. I didn't listen much, and tuned out completely when some kid said something about sailing and Nantucket. I was watching Caroline raise her food to her mouth when I heard Carlton's voice.

"So, Jack, play much football down in the city?"

"Not a lot," I said, which was not a lie. "A little wide receiver." Okay, *that* was.

Well, no, come to think of it, I *was* a pretty little wide receiver.

Outside, after dinner, I caught up to Caroline as she walked toward the girls' dorm.

"Hey," I said. "How about that Simon kid?"

"Yeah, did you see the look on Carlton's face?" she said. "Maybe it's a defense mechanism or something, until he figures the place out. Like a porcupine throwing its needles."

Or a girl being shy.

Old-style lamps half lighted the path we were walking on. She looked pretty in the dim light. Not glamorous, but . . . cool. She had brown hair, but her eyes were blue, and I could see the lamplight in them when she looked me in the face, which didn't happen enough.

"So how'd you end up at Oakhurst Hall?" I asked her.

"My high school was supposed to be in the top five best

public schools in America, or something. But it was just a bunch of cliques, and bored rich kids doing heroin and coke, and teachers who hated their jobs because they couldn't afford to drive the cars the kids they were teaching drove. Last year my class president was fencing credit cards on school computers. The baseball captain totaled his Jaguar into the school goalposts."

I kept my mouth shut, because it was kind of dry.

"The worst thing," she said, loosening up, "was that being smart and getting good grades wasn't cool. At least here there might be kids who are smart and don't feel ashamed of it. Plus, this place looked so beautiful. The mountain and the fields. What about you?" she said.

Tough question. I took the easy way out. "It wasn't my idea at first," I said. "But when I got in, I figured it'd be stupid not to try it. I kind of felt like I was running in place back home."

She smiled. "I *love* running. But so far it's been a drag. I thought cross-country would mean I could run through the woods! But it turns out you have to keep running so hard that it all just goes by in a blur."

I decided not to tell her that I liked running, too. It might sound like I was saying we should run together. Plus I could tell just by the way she'd said it that she was a real runner. Not like someone who did it for some sort of weird therapy.

We were standing in front of another one of those Gothic

stone dorms. And she didn't run away. "What'd you think of the summer reading?"

"I guess I should have done it, huh?"

"I *loved* it. You should check it out."

She looked over her shoulder and smiled a small smile. Then she jogged up her dorm steps like a runner and disappeared inside the wooden door. I just stood there, savoring something.

Then the skies opened up, which was a definite omen for the Scoville 4 dorm meeting in the Wards' living room in the apartment at the end of the hall. The walls and tables were covered with pictures of their kids, and their parents, and their barefoot wedding in a field full of flowers, and dogs. Lots of dogs.

Josh planted himself in a corner chair next to a table piled with golf books. I dropped to the floor with my back to a yellow wall. Three other kids crammed themselves onto a plaid couch and were punching one another in the arms when Ward came in, holding a bottle of Heineken in one hand.

"Hey, idiots, cut it out!" Ward yelled. Then he calmed down and took a sip of the beer. "Okay. Most of you know the drill. This is my home, and you are my guests. So let's not get off on a bad foot here. Scoville 4 is my turf. But," he said, now looking somewhere else, "I'm here for you."

"So does that mean we can drink your booze and get

back the porn you ripped off from us?" said one of the couch kids. They all looked the same to me—kind of dumb. "Can we get in on the poker game tonight?"

His buddies snickered until Ward stared them all down, and it got quiet.

"Let's make this quick," said Ward, doing that slow-motion golf swing thing again. "This year, I'm gonna be a fucking *Nazi*. Big Brother Is Watching. Bottom line? You're fifth formers now. No excuses for messing up. I don't want to have to explain to Carlton why this dorm is a bunch of losers. Which right now, as I look around, it is."

"You said the *F* word, Mr. Ward," said another couch kid. "Ten pushups."

Ward's face turned red. "That's the first demerit of the year."

Then he closed the door.

"Thanks for the vote of confidence, loser," said Josh, before we all piled back down the hallway.

I didn't want to go back and bitch and moan with Josh. I was still thinking of Caroline Callahan, and I wanted to savor the buzz. I hopped down the stairs and went outside. The rain had stopped. I could smell wet leaves, and that was good.

In the soft air, I felt a hint of freedom.

Now all I had to do was find something to do with it.

Josh was a stoner scientist. Simon was a wiseass genius who knew exactly who he was. Me? Composer of a couple hundred song fragments. Good at the piano, but only when someone else wrote what I played.

In a good song, they say "it has a hook." It was time to write a hook for myself.

JARVIS, THE ENGLISH TEACHER, WAS PROBABLY forty, but he had this look in his eyes like someone who'd been around for a hundred years. He was wearing a yellow Oxford shirt with a frayed, unbuttoned collar whose tips turned up like the chips in Mexican restaurants. With one hand he was holding a marker in front of a whiteboard, and he held a coffee mug that said OHIO TURNPIKE in the other.

Instead of desks, Jarvis's room was filled with totally weird furniture: old stuffed easy chairs, a couple of discarded dining-room chairs with Oakhurst crests on them, a blue wooden bench that looked like it was from a Little League dugout, and a fancy couch, which, by the time I came into the room, three A-listy girls had already claimed.

A desk in the corner was piled with a half dozen books about Zen Buddhism and what looked like about three years' worth of ungraded papers, even though the year hadn't even started. An old white plastic boom box from somewhere like Kmart sat on a windowsill playing early Clash.

I went for a wooden chair. A Korean boy and girl sat

next to each other on the baseball bench. Then Caroline came in, eyes to the floor. She sat next to the two Korean kids on the bench.

Suddenly, Jarvis scrawled something on the board like he was attacking it. He was writing so hard that the marker slipped out of his hand and flew over his shoulder. The Korean boy snatched it from the air, without changing the deadpan expression on his face. Some of the kids applauded. The kid stood, bowed in all directions, and handed the marker back to Jarvis, who was smiling.

"Okay. I'm Mr. Jarvis, and this is what we're going to talk about all year," he said, pointing at what he'd written. I couldn't read it.

"Albanian jumnys?" said the Korean girl.

"American journeys," said Jarvis. "We will not be identifying subordinate clauses, dangling participles, or gerundive phrases. If you don't know what those are, I believe you've all been issued grammar books, which I won't assign anything from. I just ended a sentence with a preposition, which tells you how much I care about grammar. We'll be spending our time taking journeys. Moving forward. Because if you stand still, you die."

A cocky kid with blond hair and a blue Oakhurst Hall blazer raised his hand and spoke without being asked to. "Mr. Jarvis, are you playing the Clash so we'll think you're cool?" A couple of A-list girls giggled.

Jarvis shot a caffeinated glance back at the kid. "You are . . . ?"

"Ted Thorn. I'm the vice president of the fifth form," he said like it was absurd that Jarvis didn't know who he was.

"Officer Thorn, there are eight hundred students here. I know about five of their names. Sometimes I can remember my own. Don't take it personally. To answer your question, I covered a Clash tour for *Rolling Stone* back in the Bronze Age. So, Mr. Thorn, did you manage to find time this summer to do the reading?"

"Sure. The Gatsby guy didn't make any sense. Who'd be unhappy if they lived in a house that big?"

"But why do you think Tom Buchanan takes a mistress who's married to a guy who owns a gas station?"

Silence. Jarvis scanned a piece of paper on his desk. "Lefferts?"

Damn. I sifted through my head for a bullshit answer.

"Maybe," Caroline said, "the author wants to point out how sometimes people in the upper class never bother to grow up and just grab whatever or whoever they want." Blushing at the attention, she added, "Like in Dreiser's *American Tragedy*, where the upper-class guy sleeps with the lower-class girl and then drowns her."

"Exactly. The American journey doesn't have to be a physical journey," Jarvis said, nodding. "It can be about growth, about being willing to change. Or choosing not to. Like Thorn. That was your name, right? As in, 'in my side'?"

The kid blushed.

Then Caroline said, "'So we beat on, boats against the current, borne back ceaselessly into the past.'"

"The last line of the book, and the best," said Jarvis, excited and amped. "Meaning?"

"Maybe," said Caroline, "that unless we try and break away, break the mold, we're doomed to repeat the old mistakes. That if you want things to change, you have to do it yourself."

Jarvis nodded. "And you are . . ."

"Caroline Callahan."

"Well, Caroline, perhaps you could tutor Mr. Lefferts for the *Gatsby* quiz before Wednesday's class."

Caroline was first out the door, head down. I was second. I caught up to her to thank her for saving my butt.

"Sure," she said before I had time to say anything, and unzipped her green pack. It had a Hello Kitty thingie hooked to the zipper. "Here," she said. It was her copy of *Gatsby*. "It's a real fast read." She hurried down the hall before I could say a word.

Bruno, in history, was a guy in his fifties with a gray crew cut, and his class was clearly going to be a bitch. No one spoke a word as we all sat down. He was not warm and fuzzy. We gathered around one table; the only faces I recognized were Simon Ridgway and the Korean girl. A super-pretty, super-preppy blond girl was actually filing her nails, which seemed stupid until, thirty seconds into the class, Bruno assigned a five-page paper—"Compare ancient Sparta to Al-Qaeda"—and when he said, "Anybody know why this is the assignment?" the blonde said, "They're both trying to bring down the superpowers of their time. Sparta wants to overthrow Athens in 456 BC; radical Arabs want to castrate the United States today."

Damn. And this was the airhead?

"Good, Lucy," said Bruno. "Santayana was right. Those who cannot remember the past are condemned to repeat it. As in ancient Athens, we are witnessing the death of a noble experiment: Democracy then, capitalism now. Nice ideas, but both forgot to factor in the human flaws."

"Like power-lust," said the Korean girl. "Like greed."

No one said anything. So I did. "I guess both of them looked good on paper." I looked at Lucy, but she was still filing her nails.

"Speaking of the paper," said Bruno, expressionless, "I need five sources. No Wiki. Due Wednesday. Double-spaced, inch-and-a-half margins, twelve-point font: Times New Roman. Broken printers are not excuses. I don't want 'em online, either. And I want big picture. I care less about the name of the Greek god of wine than knowing why they *had* a god of wine. Anyone?"

"Because grapes and olive oil were their major crops," said Simon. "And drinking wine makes you feel a lot better when you're being invaded than drinking olive oil. And Dionysus was a much cooler god than the god of olive oil. Was there one of those?"

"There was a god of everything," Bruno said. "Back then, people didn't know that their fate could be in their own hands. In Egypt, they thought that the gods ran everything, and that they couldn't veer from the path that the gods had given them. They were wrong. All right, good day, ladies and gentlemen."

"Sir?" Lucy said. "Class just started."

"Then I suggest you head to the library and start researching the paper."

I figured Bruno wasn't going to accept *Spartan Slaydown: Tears for Spears* as a source.

I had hated science before, and it didn't look like anything was going to change at Oakhurst Hall. The bio teacher was about twenty, totally out of it, a complete weirdsmobile. One of his sideburns was an inch longer than the other, and his tie had about seven stains on it. "Biology isn't a science here," he said. The class was a lab, stainless steely and creepy. "It's about the world. You'll learn the things you have to learn, and I hope you learn them quickly, so that we can spend more time out in the ponds and swamps."

At least he was harmless. The French teacher, Booth, looked like an intern at *Vogue*, with all the right clothes and too much of all the right makeup. She spent most of the class talking about how much she'd loved her trip to some château over the summer, throwing in a bunch of French words like *charcuterie*. Then, in the middle of her story, she suddenly yelled at Simon for putting his feet on a chair. She went totally schizoid, and started ranting about how we weren't little kids anymore and it was going to be a long year if we didn't take her classroom seriously. Then she turned back into the other person, and finished her story about sun and cheese and grapes.

"Last year was her first year out of Hamilton," Simon told me after the class. "Didn't have a clue what to do with her life, so naturally, she gets a job teaching at her alma mater. Guarantee she spends the whole year taking her failures out on us. She can *baizer mon arse*."

Intro to calculus completely went over my head. "I didn't get half of that," I said to Spencer. "What the hell's calculus?"

"It's very simple," he said. "Newton knew that certain celestial forces could not be explained by simple algebra. Should you need tutoring," he said, "feel free to ask. My fees are competitive: Twenty dollars an hour."

"You're serious?"

Spencer wiped his glasses on his tie. "I'm always serious. I fail to see what purpose humor serves, evolutionarily."

There seemed to be a lot of people around here who felt that way.

THE GYM WAS A HUGE, MODERN building that looked like a long egg carton and had been designed by someone from Finland. A bronze lion statue stood in front of it looking angry. I saw a hockey rink, four basketball courts, two pools, and a dozen glass-walled squash courts before I found the football locker room.

And—damn—there was Ward himself, standing at the door wearing a blue and gold Oakhurst Hall warm-up suit and an Oakhurst Hall baseball cap, so you couldn't tell he was going bald. He looked at his clipboard like he'd never seen me before.

"Lefferts . . . receiver? You catch passes?"

"Yeah," I said. Because I did. Well, I'd caught one here, and lots in the Giants' parking lot.

"JVs and thirds locker room. Locker thirty-four. That's your number. Grab some cleats from the pile. Be down on the field by the pond in ten minutes. Not eleven. Not twelve. Ten. Or don't show up at all."

I had to walk through the varsity locker room where four blue leather couches surrounded a blue and gold Oakhurst

Hall emblem on the carpet. A huge flat-screen was tuned to the NFL Network.

The JV locker room was small, with cinderblock walls and a cement floor. Pipes zigzagged across the ceiling. I pulled a pair of cleats out of a canvas laundry hamper and found 34: blue jersey, gold pants with the knees wearing thin. On the top shelf of the locker sat a scuffed white helmet. On the floor were some shoulder pads, some socks, and a T-shirt. On a hook, a jock with 34 Sharpied on it. I changed into the jock, and somehow I got it right on the first try. The pants felt good—tight, like a second skin. I put on the T-shirt, then pulled the shoulder pads over my head. I adjusted the straps under the arms. The jersey went over the pads. It was too loose, but it was sort of cool to have my own number, even if it had been someone else's the year before.

I hooked a finger into the face guard of the helmet. It was a lot heavier than it looked. Then I followed a group of kids out a back door, down across the main field with light towers like those machines from *War of the Worlds*. The hillside on the home side was empty, like the stands on the opposite side, at the foot of the mountain. But the field looked primed. The lines had been chalked into a perfect grid, and the end zones had been painted blue and gold.

Then we went down a path through the woods, to a field next to a large pond where Jarvis was herding about

three dozen of us into groups. I hadn't seen Jarvis as a foot-
ball-coach type. But that was cool. At least it wasn't Ward
back up with the big boys. Next to him stood a young teacher I hadn't seen. He looked outdoorsy.

"Welcome to the JVs and thirds," Jarvis said. "There
might still be a few slots up on the varsity, but for you JVs,
I'm your coach, and Mr. Devin here will coach the thirds.
We may not be the varsity, but that doesn't mean we don't
play real football. But don't forget: you're supposed to have
some fun here. So let's get going. Linemen, linebackers, over
there with Mr. Devin. Quarterbacks, running backs, receivers, defensive backs, over here with me. Let's do it."

I put my helmet on my head, felt it pinch my temples,
and tugged it down—and suddenly I was in another place,
like I'd shifted into a different world or something. Shut off
from the outside. I couldn't see to either side. The face guard
masked half the front. The smell was plastic and dried sweat.
I could hear myself taking breaths. It was like there was the
rest of the world and then there was me, in my own little
space. Like it was a real helmet. A battle helmet. Like the
shoulder pads were armor.

"Thirty-four! Hey! Huddle up! Get in here!"

I trotted into the pack of receivers. Jarvis explained the
drill: three quarterbacks were throwing to six receivers and
three running backs. I was last in line for the receivers. I
watched the kids ahead of me. Some caught the ball. Some

dropped it. A few tripped over their own feet. Some of the throws were good, some sucked.

Then it was my turn. My quarterback was number 2, a tiny kid about five foot four. Seriously. His helmet looked about eleven sizes too big for his head.

"Okay, Lefferts," said Jarvis. "Square out, ten yards."

"Right," I said. "Square out."

"Run ten yards, turn right. And a yard is three feet, in case you were wondering."

The little kid's pass was behind me and low, so I reached back and, somehow, caught the ball a few inches off the ground. It seemed to stick to my hands.

I might actually be able to do this.

On the next round, I ran a buttonhook: five yards straight downfield, turn around. But when I turned around, the little kid's pass was flying way over my head. I reached up with my right hand and tipped the end of the ball into the air. It twirled around, came down, and I caught it.

"Good concentration, thirty-four!" shouted Jarvis. Pure luck was more like it. On the third round, the receivers ran a flat-out bomb route: "Just run your balls off, as far as you can, as fast as you can," said Jarvis.

I figured there was no way the little kid could throw it far. So I sprinted full speed for thirty yards, then looked back over my shoulder—and the pass was a perfect spiral, but it was going to be too long. Then, and I don't know why, time slowed down again. And I remember thinking how amazing it was that such a little kid could throw such a good pass. Maybe that's why when I dove flat-out and stuck my hands out, the ball landed in them: I hadn't been thinking about catching it.

As I ran back to the group, it was like something had shifted a little inside me. This was something *I* did. This was something *I could do.* Even though nobody had ever told me I should do it.

"Lefferts," said Jarvis. I wasn't a number anymore. "Where'd you play last year?" The rest of the kids had gathered in a loose semicircle.

"I didn't play last year," I said.

The laughs were stopped by Jarvis's voice. "Well, you've got one hell of a pair of hands." He looked at his clipboard. "Let's try some line drills."

For the next ten minutes, I tried to learn how to get hit without getting hurt. Most of the time I got bowled over on my ass. But some of the time, the Outward Bound stuff did its work, and I stayed on my feet. And a few times, if I timed it right, I was suddenly standing over a kid I'd just knocked down. Okay, they were probably ninth graders, but that power was in there somewhere.

Finally, Jarvis called for five sprints from one end of the field to the other.

The little quarterback whined, "Five? That's five hundred yards!"

"Good math, two," said Jarvis.

The other coach, Devin, ran with us. The first two

hundreds were easy. By the middle of the third, Devin led the pack. There were only four or five kids within ten yards of him. By the fourth leg, though, I was the only kid near him. When I pivoted at the goal line for the final hundred, I caught a glimpse of the sun off the pond and flashed back to the Reservoir at home and suddenly forgot how much it hurt.

I caught Devin at the fifty. The coach looked over, smiling—and notched it up a gear. But I passed him. In the end zone, I bent over, gasping. Devin high-fived me.

On the long walk back from the pond, Jarvis told us to be sure not to walk on the varsity field, with its perfect grass and its heavy soundtrack: crunching pads, grunts, Ward's drill-sergeant screams.

Standing next to him was a bald man in a sweat suit, watching the team: Bruno. The history guy.

Suddenly, Jarvis was loping up beside me.

"Goddamn." He laughed a friendly laugh. "Too bad you weigh ninety pounds. You got better hands than anybody on the V."

"I got a lot to learn," I said.

"Yeah, well," said the English teacher, "football ain't rocket science, Jack. The less you think, the better. Take some spare time to practice catching, if you can. You might even have some fun."

"I just did," I said, and the words were unfamiliar, but I liked the way they sounded.

"PLEASE, PLEASE—I'D LIKE TO HEAR SOME nuance," Hopper said, cutting me off in mid-measure of a Mozart scherzo. He stood staring out the window of the practice room. "You do know what *nuance* means, don't you, Jack?"

Where was the kindly old guy from registration day? I guess now that they had us trapped up here, they could all summon the dark side.

"Yeah," I said. "Sure." Terrific. Music is the one thing that cools me out, and this dude was already warping it.

This is how the piano thing happened: My thumbs and pinkies can span nine notes, which is one more than an octave, which is unusual. Also for some reason, I can listen to a keyboard solo from the Old Days, like Steve Winwood or Stevie Wonder, just once, and play it back note for note within a couple of seconds. Some people are good at languages or building seawalls made of garbage. I'm good at parroting notes.

I hadn't found any modern music I really liked, because it all just sounded like the songs they play at the beginning or the end of cable TV shows, and those usually don't have keyboard parts anyway. I liked jam bands because they went in all kinds of directions, so they were bound to hit on original-sounding stuff, but there are only so many thirteen-minute Trey Anastasio solos you can listen to.

Anyway, in sixth grade, my piano teacher had said that I showed "unusual promise," and two days later, I was taking private lessons from a "top-top" Juilliard faculty guy, but all he taught me were these songs from three hundred years ago that seemed like the music was written for the kind of dances you see in those movies where everyone has wigs and Keira Knightley wears gowns. They sounded like they'd been written by a math software program. You could predict every measure.

Then one day a piano showed up in our living room— not that any of our rooms ever looked lived in—and that was kind of the game changer. It was a pretty old secondhand Steinway, but it made me feel like I had new hands or something. If I pressed the keys one way, the sound came back one way. If I pressed differently, the sound came back different. It was kind of like the keys and I were talking. They were ivory, which wasn't cool, but I'd never actually seen an elephant's tusks, so it didn't bother me a lot.

I just couldn't find anything I wanted to play on it. Anything that was my own.

So I practiced songs written by a lot of really, really, really old guys, pieces with names like "Moonlight Sonata," and half the time, I was glad to get to the end. I liked the blues best. Well, I liked the sound of them. But the blues of a rich kid from Park Avenue aren't, like, really all that . . . blue.

This time I made it through about five measures before the voice sliced through the music. "I want to hear some *articulation*," the guy said, turning slowly, for effect. "Lefferts, let's get something straight here. I don't care about your technique. Technique is a given at Oakhurst Hall. But soul? Soul is not a given. I'd like to hear some soul. You do have a soul, don't you, Lefferts?"

What was this, a cult? Break the kid down until he's a robot? If this guy was so good, what was he doing at a prep school? And taking out the frustrations of his stupid life on me?

Although, at the moment, he did have a point: I was playing badly. I was nervous. Walking down the carpeted hall lined with photographs of kids from the past, none smiling, had sort of freaked me out. Classical musical riffs— brass, string, winds—were leaking out from behind every heavy door, each with a small, thick-glassed square window. Kind of like death row cells, only in a luxury prison.

And in Hopper's studio, it didn't help that I could hear someone perfectly playing all those crazy hammering chords from Tchaikovsky's first piano concerto, even through the supposedly soundproofed wall.

"Lefferts?" Hopper said, bringing me back to the moment. "Are you with us?"

"Sorry," I said. "I was just listening to that Tchaikovsky. Pretty good, huh?"

"Yes," said Hopper. "Mario Miles is quite technically proficient. Now, please resume."

This time I hit the keys too hard, like I was pushing a goddamned doorbell. Hopper let me finish the piece as he stared out the window.

"We can call it a day," he said. "Or"—he turned around, took off his glasses, and wiped them with the broad end of his tie—"we can call it a year. We can terminate this relationship right now. It doesn't feel to me like you're putting any joy into this."

Well, where, exactly, was I supposed to find it?

He put his glasses on again, and all I could see were the gray caterpillars of his eyebrows. "I will say this once. I do not give lessons at Oakhurst Hall because I need the work. I give lessons in the hope that my students will take their music as seriously as their predecessors did. You do know who has sat on that bench before you, I trust?"

Yeah, those stiffs out in the photographs. "Yes, I do. Believe me, sir. I do. I want to get better. I really do. I mean, find joy."

"Then next week," said Hopper, "when we begin to prepare your audition piece, we will both be on the same page, so to speak. I trust that you will have chosen your piece by next week?"

"Yessir. You trust right." My audition piece? Jesus. What *was* this Thanksgiving concert? The Grammys? The Super Bowl?

I shot out into the hallway just as the door opened across the hall. The Tchaikovsky kid had a mop of seventies hair and an intense-looking face. He was wearing a black T-shirt with the Anarchy symbol on the front in white, black pants, black high-tops, and a black backpack slung over his shoulder. He was thin, without any muscles. "You must be Lefferts. I've got Latin. Let's walk." We started down the hall. "They've probably told you about me," said Mario Miles. He had the feel of a kid who knew that the best way to deal with being on Oakhurst Hall's social fringe was to pretend to not give a shit.

"Yeah, some," I said.

"All bad, I hope?" Mario laughed. "I'm not as weird as they told you. Just a little . . . competitive. But then, you'd better be competitive in this place, right? As if Mikhail Tamarovich would have won at Leeds in '99 if he'd gone to Choate or Groton."

All I knew about Leeds was it was the Who's best live album. "I don't know if I'm really in it for prizes," I said.

"Well, you are. You know McGregor? The admissions guy? His wife's family helps endow the Van Cliburn. They invented, like, the paper clip or something. So Carlton's going to get Oakhurst Hall a VC if it kills him. Can't have a wife on campus who founded the Van Cliburn without winning one of your own. That's why I got a full ride three years ago. Haven't been First Piano at Thanksgiving yet. It's make-or-break for this sicko."

He smiled. I couldn't tell what kind of smile it was. Then he said, "May the best man win." We'd reached the heavy glass entrance doors to the building. Mario stepped ahead, opened the door like a comic doorman: *"Maestro."* Then he skipped down the first few granite steps, stopped, and looked back. "So what're you gonna play for your audition piece? Hopper thinks I'm gonna try the Rach 3 and make a fool of myself, so he can gloat and give it to you or some Korean enfant terrible who studied under whoever Korea's Glenn Gould is. He thinks I'm addicted to the Russkies. But hell, how could you *not* be?"

"Sure," I said. "Right."

"But I'm gonna trip him up and go modern: Prokofiev's second piano concerto, the third movement. Early twentieth-century classical—that's where the money is, right? So what's yours?"

I tried to be cool. "Maybe Beethoven's seventh, second movement."

· · ·

"The infamous Mario Miles." Caroline had come out of the music building behind us, carrying a flute case. "What were you guys talking about?"

"My 'audition piece,'" I said. "So I guess this concert is big, huh?"

She sat down on the staircase. I was right next to her a second later.

"First Piano tours with the symphony over spring break in Europe," she said. "My flute teacher said last year a kid named Ji-Hoon got it because Hopper taught him, and Mario doesn't need a teacher. Everyone here is so scary good, right? We're doing this thing Mendelssohn wrote when he was sixteen. You would not believe the other kids. I don't think they get it, but they play it." She checked her watch. "Oh, jeez. I'm late for Spanish." She jumped to her feet.

I loved that: *Oh, jeez.*

"So how was your first lesson with Hopper?" she asked as we started to walk.

"Way intense," I said. "I guess they forgot to tell me I was at Juilliard, and we're playing Carnegie Hall at Thanksgiving. He didn't like my 'articulation.' And I didn't like the way he talked."

We'd reached the languages building. "So, have you read *Gatsby* yet?" she said.

"Yeah. I finished it last night." I actually had, sort of. At least, I'd read all the sentences she'd purpled, and her notes in the margins. She had that girl handwriting where you can read everything really clearly, and all the letters look like little happy cartoon characters.

"See ya," she said, disappearing into the language building.

"Hope so," I said.

Lame.

"'AND IF THINE EYE OFFEND THEE, pluck it out.' That's from the Sermon on the Mount, of course. The Book of Matthew. Chapter eighteen, verse nine."

Carlton's voice bounced around the huge chapel. He was on this little stage like those cherry pickers that electrical workers stand in, only with wooden carvings on the bucket. I'd been in a church only three or four times, as a little kid, when Mom and Dad were together. But this one smelled just like the one in New York ten years ago. Sort of dead.

"Now, do we really believe that Jesus was suggesting that a man whose eyes have coveted another's wife should blind himself? Was Our Savior actually encouraging the sinner to *pluck out his own eye?*"

"Eeew," said the girl in the pew in front of me: Lucy, the blonde from history. It was eight forty-five, right after Sunday breakfast. I was dying for anything from the Starbucks on Seventy-Eighth and Lex, where Luke would be meeting a few other kids about five hours from now, after they all woke up.

The seating was alphabetical. I was in a small, two-seat pew up against a stone wall, beneath a large stained-glass window of a saint who didn't look happy. The kid next to me was the Korean kid from English class. The first week in class, he hadn't said a word. The only time he'd moved was to catch Jarvis's marker. If his eyes hadn't been open, you'd have thought he was sleeping.

". . . Or was Jesus's message more figurative, do you think?" Carlton said. "Isn't it likelier that the Son of God was speaking metaphorically? And so, as we assemble on a glorious Sunday morning two millennia later, I ask, what can we learn from His words today?"

Staring straight ahead, the Korean kid suddenly whispered, "We can learn that, verily and forsooth, we must continuously wander in bountiful gratitudosity through the Holy Plains of hallowed St. Oakhurst Hallshire-on-New-Hampshire-downs, casting neither seed nor sin against the righteous hallowed sod. Amen."

I looked at him. He didn't look back. He kept talking, though, just loud enough for me and the girl and guy in front of us to hear.

"But, O Lord, let us not take for granted the holy fish sticks and the plentiful French fries and the limitless tartar sauce. Nor shall we overlook those female faculty for whom we are eternally lustful. For all of which, O Lord, we remain eternally grateful. All the best, sincerely, et cetera, amen."

Slowly, the kid turned his face and looked at me. "Sam," he whispered.

"What?"

"They call me Sam."

"That's your name?"

"No, but Oak prefers we all be Western," he said, straight-faced, looking back toward the pulpit. "And I'm a Sammy Davis Jr. fan."

Lucy turned around. Suddenly I had all these stupid thoughts: Did I have bed head? Did my tie match my shirt? Did I care whether she cared? Nope. She was sort of card-boardy. But eye candy tastes good no matter what it's made of, right?

". . . that it is not only a sin to *commit* an improper act, but to *think* of doing so. The message? Turn toward the good, turn away from temptation." Now Carlton's voice went from preacher to headmaster. "And, as I'm sure some of you see where I'm going with this, you must ignore the temptation of looking at anyone's paper but your own. Whether that paper is on the next desk or on the internet."

"Ah—the Gospels of Google," whispered Sam. "Our annual Plagiarism Parable. Interesting. Last year it was Revelations."

"You'll be hearing from the dean on this in detail," Carlton droned on, "tomorrow, at our annual ethics orientation. Mandatory attendance. Just keep in mind that cut-and-paste scholarship is something we take very seriously at Oakhurst Hall. Forewarned is forearmed."

"And foreskinned," said Sam, deadpan, just loud enough to make Lucy giggle.

The organ swung into a hymn. We all shot to our feet, me last. Sam opened a hymnbook and began to sing. Like everyone, he seemed to have a great voice. I grabbed a hymnal with a cracked red-leather binding from the shelf in the back of Lucy's pew and joined in. And out of the blue, I started feeling the Gothic vibe of the song, and the heaviness of the melody, and the way the damned minor-key seriousness hit me over the head: how sometimes music can make you feel like nothing else does. The notes hit your brain in a place reserved just for hearing music. Right up to the "ah-men," with its descending half note.

As bells started to ring from the tower, I peeled off into the aisle, but Sam grabbed my jacket sleeve. Apparently you had to leave the place in order. As Lucy passed my pew, she said, without looking at me, "You were flat."

"So what's with the plagiarism thing?" I asked Sam. We were walking back up to the main campus on a winding pathway bordered by well-trimmed bushes.

"Last year a Korean kid put a few paragraphs from *On the Road* into a short story," he said. "Not like your teacher wouldn't notice that suddenly you were writing like Jack Kerouac on speed, right? But they let it go. Jarvis convinced the dean that you gotta give us some leeway. The Korean clan.

The year before, he even got them to stop giving us demerits for speaking Korean in the hallways."

Sam turned to extend his hand for me to shake. He was smiling for the first time, like the Michelin Man. "Glad to meet you officially. I'm Sang-Ook Lim, member of the tortured Korean subculture, Northeastern Prep School branch."

"Jack Lefferts," I said. "Member of the overprivileged American branch. New York division."

"I've met members of your tribe before," Sam said. "They are plentiful here."

"So why's it tougher on you guys?" I said, and we started to walk again.

"The Ivies have a Korea quota, right?" said Sam. "They definitely want to fill it, 'cause we're supposed to be super-students. But no college wants to have more Koreans than honkies. We have to get straight A's to get one of the slots. Pile up the extracurriculars, play in the symphony, tutor inner-city kids in Concord. I'm treasurer of the Campus Organic Garden Club. And if I myself don't get into Harvard, my best option will be to pluck out my *own* eyes and jump into the River Han. That's in the middle of soulless Seoul. Without the MBA, how can I possibly manage the food biz back home?"

"Your family has a grocery store?"

"You could say that. My family owns, like, all the food

in Korea, or something. If you ever need a deal on six billion bucks' worth of soybeans, text my dad." He laughed. Then, out of the blue, he said, "So what'd you think about the Man's sermon?"

This caught me off guard. I hadn't given it much thought. "If he means I can't think about Lucy while he's babbling, I can't agree."

"Better stay away from that one, son," Sam said. "That's the varsity quarterback's babe. Vic Madden's a god. The girl is a Muffy."

"A what?"

"What, you never read *The Preppy Handbook*? It's required in Seoul schools before they ship us here to be indoctrinated. Muffy. Biff. The perfect prepazoids."

"Like I'd have a chance with Lucy anyway." Like Caroline didn't blow her away, anyway.

"Hell," Sam said. "That wasn't even the best story about plucking out your eyes. *X: The Man with the X-Ray Eyes*. Roger Corman, 1963. Ray Milland invents X-ray vision, but seeing everything drives him insane—it's too much to take. Like, raw humanity is too gross. So he pulls his eyeballs out. Awesome. Check it out between your Hopper lessons."

"How do you know I play piano?"

"You're new meat." His face erupted into a happy cupcake kind of look. "Everyone knows everything about you. Including how you're gonna give Mario Miles a run for his money for the First Piano slot. Or, to put it another way, everyone *hopes* you're gonna give Miles a run for his money."

"How come?" I said. "Is he an asshole?"

"Nah. Just a kid with an IQ of about 400, with the scholarship chip on his shoulder and about eleven learning disabilities they haven't even invented yet. He doesn't run with a pack. It makes everyone else think he's weird."

Josh caught up with me after dinner. "Forget the homework tonight, stud. Time for your audition for the band." Sounded good.

"If this was a string quartet, they'd give us our own practice room. Hell, we'd have our own faculty adviser," my roommate said, leading me through a back door of the arts building with a key he wasn't supposed to have. In a practice room stuffed with extra chairs and music stands that no one supposedly used, a tall kid with blond hair just long enough to meet the hair code was fingering the neck of his bass. Simon Ridgway was randomly bopping the tom-tom of the drum kit: I guess the wiseass had passed Josh's audition.

"Danny, Simon, this is Jack the Piano Man," Josh said, lighting a joint. He took a hit, and started passing it around. I passed. Then I sat down at a thirties Steinway upright. It had chipped keys and stains on the wood, but a Steinway's still a Steinway. When I tried a few chords, it was like the keys were smiling back at me.

Josh strummed some simple chords on his guitar, and the other two kids fell into the rhythm. I picked up on the chord progression, but I didn't add much to the tune.

"You have a real nice touch," Danny said, but his eyes were darting around the room. Then Simon started this mean hard snap on the drums, and Josh ripped some power chords, and Danny added a heavy bass. I couldn't add anything, and their mini jam died out. So I began to play the first thing that came to my mind: a simple, minor chord progression from a Schubert thing from seventh grade that sort of sounded just like Danny's bass line.

"That's from Fantasy for Four Hands, right?" Danny said. "Second movement?"

"You play classical?"

He smiled. "Naw, my dad used to write music textbooks. I dug the pictures of the old guys. I wasn't a gamer like everyone else, so I started teaching myself some of what they wrote. Played a little piano til I heard Jack Bruce playing for Cream. Got bit by the bass and never looked back. Going for Berklee. Let's try it again."

I repeated the Schubert, and in a weird way, it sounded like a good fit, just the chords playing with Danny's bass line. Simon put down his sticks and picked up some brushes and began to massage his snare. Josh waterfalled a bunch of quiet lead notes. All of a sudden, we were playing something.

Then I shifted into a different progression, using some sort of lizard-brain-muscle-memory from all the years of music-theory classes—but not a predictable one; sort of a progression you couldn't see coming. The other guys fell into step with it really quickly. And they could *play*.

A minute later, we were actually . . . *composing* something. On the other hand, they were all stoned by now, and the thing we were trying to write just died on the vine.

"I think we have the beginnings of something there," Josh said, and he was right: that was all we had. But instead of trying again, he lit another joint.

This time Danny passed too. "That octave figure you played, with the tritones?" he said to me. "I expected fifths. Very cool. Now let's try making it a little spookier." He started up the bass line again, only with a few new minor-key digressions, playing with the timing. And this time, for a full three minutes, the thing sounded as if it made sense. Then we all went off down our own paths for a few seconds, but somehow, we all veered back to the same place, to a nice ending. It was like going through the rapids on some river on Outward Bound, where after you go through the ruffly stuff, you land in a calm pool.

Josh was smiling his stoner smile. "Who says it all has to be rock, right? I was getting sort of tired of Nirvana anyway."

• • •

"Jack's on the football team," Josh said as we all walked back. "Boy wonder."

"JV," I said.

"Seriously?" Danny said. "You sure don't look like a meatstick to me. Your neck isn't wider than your head. And I sure hope you don't dip."

I'd tried dipping once, and puked into the flowers in the middle of Park Avenue.

"Madden? The quarterback?" said Josh. "Guy dips so much he had to have his gums scraped three times last season. At least foliage doesn't turn your gums black."

"What about you?" I asked Simon.

"Sports? Midnight sledding. As soon as the snow hits, I'm gonna borrow a cafeteria tray and hit the backside of the mountain."

"Just don't get frostbite on your fingers," Josh said. "We need them on the snare. Lead with your head."

THE NEXT DAY, HEADING TO FOOTBALL practice, I was crossing the carpet in the main locker room when Ward called out, "Lefferts! You and Garver are up with the varsity today. Main field. Ten minutes. Not eleven. Ten. If you're not there in ten, don't bother joining the big boys. Just keep on walking to the pond. Then keep walking into it."

It was good to know that Ward the coach was as much of an asshole as Ward the dorm-master. That gave me twice as many chances to learn how to play his psycho game.

In the JV locker room, a short, muscular kid stuck out his hand. "Anthony Garver. Bronx, New York. Future Hall of Famer. I guess they're giving us a tryout, huh? So were you serious down with the jayvees? About how you never played?"

Anthony was sort of built like a bowling ball. He was a running back who'd broken a bunch of tackles in that first practice. "Yeah. What about you?"

"Played the game all my life. Pop Warner, Optimists, Catholic League, all that shit. Mom always told me sports'd be my ticket out. I got in here on Prep for Prep. 'Givin' the underprivileged a chance.' So now I got a chance to learn Latin. Shit. Where I live, Latino'd be more useful."

We walked down to the field together. "So we get to meet Bruno," Garver said.

"I already did," I said. "He's my history teacher. Doesn't smile much. He the assistant?"

Anthony stopped. "Dude, he's the *head*. New guy. He just lets Ward do all the talking." Anthony explained that Carlton was so desperate to win the championship after losing it for cheating that he'd demoted Ward and gone outside the box to snag Bruno, a guy from Real Football World. He'd been a head coach at a D-III in Pennsylvania until his career had flamed out because he punched a player on the sideline after the kid had fumbled in a big game. Then he'd had to take a high school gig in coal country, where he won two championships before he got the call from Carlton.

"But Bruno'll do the thinking, so we get real football, not wuss football." Anthony said. "He runs a pro-style offense. Lots of passes. And Madden has the arm. He's the real thing. Maybe we get the trophy and we get to keep it. Tell you this: I'm not going back down to that lake."

The trophy was for whatever league we were in, which was something like, I swear, the NEFISC. If we won it, I guessed we'd be kings of the world.

· · ·

Ward started screaming at some straggling players ambling down the hill to the varsity field. "Let's go! Let's go, girls!"

Nice.

Bruno stood next to Ward. This time he wasn't a history teacher. He was a head coach. You could tell just by the way he stood. His arms were folded across his chest. His feet were planted into the ground, like a statue. He kept his mouth closed, but his eyes were darts. I liked that he wasn't wearing an Oakhurst Hall sweatshirt or an Oakhurst Hall cap. Just jeans, a gray sweatshirt with no logo, and a John Deere baseball cap that looked like he'd worn it driving a tractor somewhere for real.

We did laps. No one talked. We did warm-up exercises. No one talked.

"Line it up!" Ward shouted. "You know the drill. Eleven-on-eleven, and I want to hear the pain."

I found the receivers and hung on the outside of the group. There were three of them.

"I'm Will Martin. Who're you?" said one, a tall black kid wearing 85.

"Jack Lefferts. I was with the JVs yesterday. You told me where my dorm was on the first day of school."

"The lost boy!"

"Still am," I said. "I've never actually played the game."

His eyes widened. "You shitting me?"

I shook my head. Martin laughed. "What am I supposed

to be, your campus guardian angel? All right, little man, just listen. When they call your number, line up, split right. And watch your ass. Don't kid yourself about this being practice. Those jerks on defense take it real serious."

The first few plays I watched were scary intense. Kids were shouting, grunting, bleeding. Madden, the quarterback, was six feet tall, muscled, swaggery, and had blond hair flipping up out of the back of his helmet, like a rock star. His running back was an ugly guy named Addison. He had muscles in his muscles. He broke tackles like a tank.

"Lefferts! Get in there!" Ward finally shouted. "It's a two sixty-seven plow right. The two back goes between the tackle and the end."

Will pushed me to the outside. "Split out five. It'll be a run to right, and you gotta seal the cornerback. Block him toward the sideline."

I lined up. Over to my left, I saw a huge guy, the right tackle, bent into his three-point stance, snorting, ready to level the defensive end facing him across the line, who was just as gigantic. About five yards in front of me, the cornerback was Thorn, the class VP, staring me down.

Madden called the signals. I had time to take about two steps before Thorn hit me chest high and slammed me over backward, just as Addison, who couldn't find a hole, ran into me from behind. Everybody went down in a heap, I was bent and folded in the middle of the pile. I felt like I'd been in a car crash.

"What the hell? What the HELL?" I was looking up into Ward's red face. It was the color of a cherry-flavored Skittle. "You call that a BLOCK? They sent you up here so you could get my best running back KILLED?" I scrambled to my feet. "You got exactly one more chance to show me what the HELL you are doing up here, buddy. I don't need receivers who can't block."

He stalked away. I looked over at Bruno. The head coach was just staring at me. Spooky. "Nice block, asshole," Addison said. He had a Southern accent. "Getcher ass back to the pond, boy." He looked like the kind of guy who'd hold up a 7-Eleven for fun.

I walked back to the sideline as Will came back out. He stopped, suddenly turned to me, bent down, and shoved his shoulder pads into my stomach, pushing me back, hard. "Like that, okay? Hit him low. Guess they didn't bring you up here for your blocking."

They ran three more plays before it was my turn again. This time, as I walked to the line, the huge tackle to my left said, in a low voice, "Dive at Thorn's legs. Bad left knee. Don't hurt him. But make him think you might." Okay. He was a jerk anyway.

At the snap, I took off toward Thorn and dove toward

his legs. He mostly dodged me, but he was out of the play just long enough for Anthony to turn up the sideline for fifteen yards before a safety shoved him out of bounds— and then shoved him again when he was off balance, and Anthony fell into a bench.

Late hit. Will was right: it was offense against defense.

"Yeah, Bannerman," shouted Zowitzki at the safety.

Ward barked at me, "Still not good enough, Lefferts. I haven't seen you hit anyone yet. They tell me you got hands. Try using 'em."

Okay, then. Everybody else was totally wired, so why shouldn't I get there? On the next play, I coiled myself and hit Thorn hard in the stomach with my helmet, then threw my right shoulder at him with everything Outward Bound had given me. It was enough to tangle him up for a second, enough for Anthony to gain a few yards behind me before some gigantic lineman shot over, moving like an elephant in *Fantasia*, and wrapped Anthony up, threw him to the ground, and thumped his chest in celebration.

"Not necessary," said a voice, all gravelly and low: Bruno. First words of the day.

"All right," Ward said. "Let's run some routes. Let's air it out." There were two quarterbacks, Madden and a kid named Griffin. The first passing drill was supposed to be no-contact. I watched the other receivers run fly patterns— straight out, forty yards. Madden had a hell of an arm. Will, running in huge loping strides, caught his first pass. The other two receivers weren't as impressive: one kid dropped the ball, and the other was too slow to catch up with Madden's long throw.

"Lefferts!" It was Ward. "Forget the bomb. Run a look-in, five yards."

I figured a look-in was what it sounded like. Will tugged at my jersey. "You're gonna get leveled. Be ready. Be cool." He smiled. "Stay healthy, little man."

"Defense!" barked Ward. "This one is full contact. I want to *hear* it. Let's *execute*."

Exactly. Ward was trying to get me killed. Maybe since he hadn't recruited me? Whatevs. I was cannon fodder, and now I knew the stakes: The next play was the difference between playing under the *War of the Worlds* light towers and screaming crowds and giggling girls, or down next to the pond, for a lot of geese.

As I lined up, I heard Jarvis's voice: *Football ain't rocket science.*

I ran out five yards, turned left, looked back, and saw the ball flying toward me. Madden had thrown the ball *way* harder than it had to be. Spiraling like a bullet heading for my chest.

I don't remember reaching out—my hands sort of did it on their own—because first I felt a helmet crack into my back, sharp, like a knifepoint, and the explosion of hurt walloped my rib cage. A flash of light came somewhere from a deep, dark place. I hit the ground on my back, and there was

Zowitzki on top of me, grinning. His breath had this weird chemical smell to it.

But the ball was between us. My hands had held on.

I tried to hop back to my feet, stumbled a little, then gained my balance. Maybe it was pure chance I'd caught it. Or maybe it *wasn't* rocket science. Maybe if your hands did the work and freed your head to get in the right place . . .

"Sweet hit, Swicky!" Thorn slapped Zowitzki's shoulder pads. As if the catch didn't matter.

Anthony came over, slapped my pads. "You okay?"

I nodded. I was *better* than okay. He offered a fist bump. I bumped him back and looked over at Bruno. He nodded at me, once. It was the highest praise I'd gotten in a long, long time.

On the second round, Ward let me run long, so I just sprinted flat out. One thing I had was speed. I blew past Thorn. He reached to grab my jersey, but I was already past him. Then, after about forty yards, I looked back over my shoulder to see the ball already falling out of the sky. Madden had led me perfectly. I didn't have time to think or worry. The ball just sort of settled into my palms.

Then I was in the end zone. I'd run seventy yards. I felt like running into the next state.

I trotted back to the rest of the team, and Garver hip-bumped me, but no one else said a thing. I looked at Madden, but he was talking with Ward.

The rest of practice was a blur of agility drills and sprints. When it was over, I barely had the strength to climb the embankment back to the locker room.

"Dude." Zowitzki was suddenly by my side. His forehead was pouring sweat, and his eyes were sort of lit up like a pinball machine. "You can take a hit. But, man, what do you weigh?"

"About one sixty, I guess." Well, maybe wearing chain-mail armor.

"More like one forty," said Zowitzki. "That's gotta change. Start lifting, like, now. Like, tonight. We never had a real passing game before. They just always double-teamed Martin. But if Bruno's thinking a passing game, you know what this could do? Having our own Wes Welker?"

Zowitzki turned to walk into the locker room, then looked back. "We should talk. Remsen 3, last room on the right. On getting you strong, dude, I am the genius. I got a personal trainer back home. From Germany. He's a very valuable guy. Very supplied. I'll show you a few options you probably haven't considered."

In the cramped JV locker room, Anthony was cleaning out his stuff. "Hey, we made it!" he said. "Ward told me we got new lockers. In the big room. The Promised Land. At least this week. He didn't tell you?" We fist-bumped again.

I'd made it? I'd made it! "Only person who told me any-thing is Zowitzki—that I have to start lifting."

Anthony laughed. "Yeah, lifting. I'm sure that's how he got that cut. Lifting. The cat is juiced. 'Roids, man. Those biceps don't come from mainlining Monster or Red Bull."

In the big room—the big room!—a kid in a T-shirt came up to us. "Lefferts, you're over there with the receivers and the linemen. Garver, over in the corner with the backs. Jocks and socks in the hamper over there."

My new locker was big, and empty.

Then the manager tossed me a new jersey: number 88. A real receiver's number.

Also, the number of keys on a Steinway.

"What do I do with this one?" I held out my 34.

"Burn it."

I turned around and put the new jersey on a hook, kind of carefully, and sat in the locker. A bruise was greening up on my right arm, and when I took a deep breath, something hurt on the right side. The sound system blared System of a Down, backed by the whoops of the players in the showers.

The big offensive tackle came over to my locker in boxers with Boston Bruins logos, toweling himself off. "Michael Clune," he said. "I guess Harris got cut, since you're in his locker, huh? Cold. Dude's on scholarship, too."

I'd never said a word to Harris. Part of me felt bad for him. But only part.

Clune turned back to his own locker, a few stalls away,

and started dressing. I saw a huge plastic jug full of large pills next to his shoes. He saw me staring.

"Vitamins," Clune said, knotting his tie. "And, hey—start lifting. Seriously. You gotta put some weight on. I kid you not. Prep football is as dirty as it comes. A good game spoiled by spoiled rich assholes. Get ready for some pain."

Down the hall, at least half the varsity was already in the weight room, and about half of them were watching themselves in the mirror that took up a whole wall. Down here it was a band I didn't recognize, with the bass up full, and kids were jackhammering the weights on the Universals in time with the beat. The smell was gaggy: not just sweat, but some lab smell.

In shorts and a T-shirt, I lay down on a black plastic bench. Over my head was a barbell with two twenty-five-pound weights on each end. Thorn was two benches away. He looked over. "That's the last time you'll ever beat me, by the way. So welcome to the jungle."

He pumped a few times, watched himself in the mirror. I couldn't help thinking that he was pretty ripped for a dickhead asshole class officer.

He started pumping. I started pumping.

"So what do you think of the tunes?" he said.

"They sort of suck," I said.

"What—As I Lay Dying? *Suck?* It's only fucking Christian heavy metal, dude! How cool is that? No emo in here, my man." He racked his own weights, then came over and slipped two more onto my bar. "That's a hundred."

I pulled off three reps, and that was all I could do. Thorn shook his head. "Hey, we need hands on this team. But no way do you stay healthy up here looking like freaking Pee-Wee Herman. Try out some mechanical squats. And the Universals. And go see Swicky. Like, tonight."

I lay back down on the bench and stared at the ceiling. My biceps were trembling. I could feel my heart thumping. Suddenly Will's goatee was hovering over me. "A hundred?"

"It was Thorn's idea."

"That figures. Here," he said, and slid some weights off the bar. "Try doing ten light reps at fifty. Easy and fluid. It's not about the weight. It's about the rhythm. Like music. You know why Phil Jackson always wanted his teams to be like the Dead? 'Cause they could jam all day and never lose the rhythm. Find the rhythm, it actually gets easier. And here, try this." He offered earphones. "Jazz. Miles Davis, live at the Blackhawk. San Francisco, 1961. Very smooth. That heavy metal shit will rot your brain."

He drifted away to a mat, where he started doing something that looked like a ballet mixed with martial arts. I smoothly did ten reps. Then added five. He came back over.

"You really think I can do this?" I said to the big kid. "I mean, I'm not even sure I know the rules of the game."

"Hell yeah," he said. "First off, you've got some athletic

chops. Raw, but still. Second, this isn't D-I. Here it's all about who wants it more. And you got those hands. Now you gotta just stand up to the pain. Look—just hit the other guy as hard as he's hitting you. Or harder. The rest of it will take care of itself." He shrugged. "Or not. Why'd you decide to start now?"

"Long story. But Martin . . ."

"Will."

"Will. What's the bug up Ward's ass?

"It's 'cause you're not one of his, and you're a musician, boy. There aren't any musician football players here. You're a *freak*. Hey, a little senior advice: if you fight this place, it just pushes back harder. Go with the flow, let it work for you. But don't let Zowitzki's boys tell you what to do. You can't catch the ball if your biceps are torn in half."

"The weights are going take some time."

Will stopped smiling. "That's not what I meant. 'Roid muscles can tear like tissue. Short-term gain, long-term pain. Do some research. Not to mention that they shrivel your dick. Then, Zowitzki's so ugly he doesn't have any use for it anyway. His hand doesn't care how shriveled his dick is."

11

THE MONOTONOUS THUD OF "SATISFACTION" FILLED the hall of
Remsen 3, the kind of song that I used to always hear coming
out of my dad's study when he'd had a couple of bottles of
high-priced grape and he was trying to get back to the days
when guys were guys and rock could live on three chords.

I passed Clune's room, with the door open. He was
sitting at a desk, wearing nothing but those Bruin boxers,
reading an Elmore Leonard novel, slapping a pencil on the
edge of his desk, in rhythm to the song.

"Where's Zowitzki's room?" I asked.

"Two doors down." Clune shouted, over the music. "And
start lifting, son. Hesford's a week from Saturday."

Zowitzki's room wasn't what I'd expected: it was as neat
as a museum gallery. Not a stray sock. The bed was made.
Textbooks were lined up like soldiers at attention beneath
his desk lamp.

"Lefferts! Glad to see you, boy." He hopped off his bed,
slammed the door shut, piled past me, dropped into his desk
chair, and, in one fluid motion, unlocked the bottom drawer
and pulled out a pile of football magazines. Beneath them I

saw rows of plastic jars of powder and prescription pill bottles and little dark jars full of liquid. They didn't have labels.

"Have a seat, boy, have a seat." He pointed to another
chair next to the bed and flicked a plastic bottle at me. Then
another. Then another. I dropped all three.

"Start with the milk stuff," said Zowitzki. He was
talking about twice as fast as most people. "Banana's not
bad. Berry's sweet. Whatever works for you. We order in
bulk. Hey! *Bulk*. Get it? Then we'll bump you up to the
serious stuff."

So that's why they always smelled like some funky
swamp in a lab beaker: he—and who else?—was sweating 'roids and supplements and who knew what from who
knew where? What did they call it in biology? Spontaneous
generation? Life from the swamp thanks to a lightning
bolt? It was Frankenstein football. How many of them took
the stuff?

"Do the shakes for two weeks," he said, "you'll put on a
ten easy. If you're not into needles, there's other ways, but
it's way painless. But believe this: none of this shit works if
you're not holdin' up your end. Do the lifting. No magic
bullets here. If I had a hundred bucks for every jerkweed
who thought it worked by itself, I'd be a rich man. You do
the work, the stuff'll do its thing."

I scanned the labels, with their cheap comic-book
graphics. It all seemed kind of lame, but I didn't want

to come off as a complete asshole. "This what everybody does?"

He frowned. "Are you kidding me? Half the league's as loaded as we are. They surf the same sites. That's where Oakhurst Hall enterprise kicks in. We do our homework, and experiment, and find the right cocktails."

"From Germany?"

"That's our competitive edge," he said, putting the magazines back.

"Does Will take supplements?"

"Martin doesn't *need* to take anything." Gross little blots of spittle were clotting at the corners of his mouth. "He's a natural. Freak of nature. He'll be all-Ivy. Martin doesn't hurt us by not being active. You, on the other hand, are no good to us at a hundred fifty pounds. You'll last about two games before they carry you off on a stretcher. Wait'll you see the linebackers from Chelton. They're monsters. I mean, literally."

"No they aren't," I said, ever the wiseass, but he was like my dad. It was just too easy. "If they were literally monsters, Zowitzki, they'd be supernatural. *Literal* means 'real.'"

He was suddenly very serious and scary. "Let's see who's at Harvard two years from now, asshole," he said, slamming the drawer. He cooled out a little as he locked it. "Lefferts, do you want to be a teammate or a solo?"

When I answered, "I just want to play football," he whipped his head back around to look at me.

"Okay. *Why?*"

It suddenly felt like a final exam. "I want to find out if I'm good at it," I said. "And my father thinks I can't."

"Right, got it. Psych 101," he said sarcastically. I'd made the mistake of thinking that a juicer couldn't also be smart. "Listen, this is bigger than what you or I want. It's about all of *us*. Read your Freud. That'd be *Civilization and Its Discontents*: act for the good of the tribe—or in this case, the school that can make us all zillionaires. And, yeah, I read more than comic books."

He got up from the chair and headed back to his bed. "Look, dude: Being on a championship team isn't about you. It's about Carlton being able to ramp up our recommendation letters for college. And it's about the ring, man. It's called *champions*."

He looked back at me, all mock earnest. "Hey, you're a moral guy. I can tell. So do some good for mankind, Gandhi. Help us out here. It's win-win."

Then he flopped back onto the bed. He was done with me. "See you in practice. Don't wuss out on me."

I stuffed the plastic bottles in my pack. Then I walked back down the hallway, to the sounds of "Jumpin' Jack Flash." Talk about museums.

. . .

But as I walked back to Screwville 4, I figured it all kind of made sense. If you've been put in a place that's supposed to give you an advantage over everyone else in the world, the pressure to pull it off is even more intense, right? So why wouldn't you reach for every bottle?

Man, I hate needles.

The Ping-Pong game sounds coming out of the common room were all weird grunts and clicks at warp speed. It was Sam and a Chinese kid, tall and skinny. I stuck my head in. The point was going on forever. Sam was smashing forehand shots, grunting each time like some Russian girl tennis player, but the Chinese kid was like a human backboard, moving back and forth, all elastic, not making a sound. You couldn't even hear his feet touch the ground as he shuttled from side to side, a good five feet behind the table, but sweat was streaming down his face, and his hair was matted to his forehead.

Finally Sam hit a smash that the other kid lunged for and couldn't reach. The kid slammed his paddle on the fireplace mantel in fury, and the paddle split in two.

Sam, meanwhile, bowed to the four walls, rotating in a circle, until he saw me.

"I am a god," Sam said.

Maybe he was. He was sure a whole lot easier to believe in than a headmaster On-High Almighty preaching out of a chapel cherry picker.

• • •

"How was your visit with your buddy Zowitzki?" Josh, sitting on the floor with his back to the radiator, was noodling a chord progression on a perfectly restored Martin D-38.

"Weird smell, weirder guy." I pulled out the bottles. "And he wants me to drink this stuff. Then shoot up steroids. Like, with a needle. That's crazy."

"No surprise there. You ever hear of 'roid rage? Never got it, myself. Where I come from drugs are supposed to make you smile, not go gonzo. On the other hand, maybe you bulk up, go Incredible Hulk, make the game-winning catch against Essex for the championship, and Lucy Prescott fulfills your every fantasy."

He strummed a chord. "Hey, listen to this." He played a few single-string notes. Real quiet. "I was thinking that could be the beginning of the piece. It kind of vibes with the old-guy chords you played that Danny liked."

It was a good melody, a catchy couplet. "When'd you write it?"

He smiled. "I didn't. It was a fucking bird. At five this morning. Singing the same four notes outside the window."

He played them again. Birdsong. "I've been overthinking this music stuff. From now on, let it flow. Speaking of which, I am about to hit the basement for a small puff. Should you care to join."

Zowitzki's mad-scientist vibe had given me the creeps. And part of me kept thinking, *I can get stoned at home. What's the point of doing Oakhurst Hall if I'm just gonna burn more brain cells?* But I followed Josh down the stairs and out the door, then around to the side of the building, where another door led down a flight of back stairs I hadn't noticed before. At the bottom, on the other side of the creaky door, lit by a red-light exit sign, was a long, dark cement hallway, about as wide as a bowling-alley lane. It reeked of leaking fuel oil, moldy plaster, and rotting wood. Cobwebs hung from pipes that looked like they were wrapped in flaking asbestos. It was like a dungeon in *Grimrock*.

Josh pushed another door open, pulled a chain on a bare lightbulb, and lit up a dusty storage room. He propped the door open with an old folding chair. "There's a stairway at each end of the hallway," he said. "We hear someone coming down one stairway, we go out the other end." He flopped onto a couch that looked new.

"Someone left that behind?" I said. I sat on a wooden classroom chair from maybe fifty years ago.

"They leave everything behind. Disposable income, disposable furniture. Sometimes I sleep on this puppy." He cracked an old window and pulled a joint from his breast pocket. I took a deep hit. The room wrapped itself in silence. I was listening for sounds out in the hallway, with stoned antennae, growing paranoid as hell.

Josh made a pot-fueled pronouncement: "So here we are, the misfit offspring of misguided parental units, and

I say, 'Deal with it. These are the cards they dealt us. So we play them.'"

I took another hit. It was stupid cotton-candy-head time again.

"I'm turning in these cards," I said. I stood up and started for the door. "Nothing personal. It's all too weird. Too many people finding the easy way out. I got history to read. See you upstairs," I said.

I went to the right and heard my steps echoing off the cement walls like in bad horror flick. I creaked open the outside door, ran up the steps into the dark night, and took a deep breath, just to get my head clear before starting to walk across the grass. Crackly, dusty leaves let loose a dusty smell: good, earthy dirt, not stoned dustiness.

Back in the room, I was starving. Then I remembered the plastic bottles. I pulled one of the supplements out of my pack and went into the bathroom, which was empty, except for the usual wet towels lying on the tiles, and bottles and tubes and crusty razors on the sinks and shelves. I filled up a smudged water glass and dumped in a couple of tablespoons of powder. I stirred it with the handle of somebody's gross toothbrush. The stuff looked like swamp scum and smelled like bananas.

What the hell: nothing ventured, nothing gained.

It didn't actually taste that bad. Like the milk at the bottom of a bowl of Lucky Charms.

But now what? That weed had been way too strong. I started to semipanic; what had I just smoked?

Josh was back in the room, sitting on the floor, working on those same four notes. I sat at my desk and cracked the history textbook. Athens. Athens? Athens was where REM came from, in Georgia, right?

Then I read the label of the bottle: *endogenous creatine precursor*—precursor to what? *Purified bovine colostrum extract*? Was that a cow's asshole?

Great. I lay on the bed, picked up *Gatsby*, tried not to pay attention to my heartbeat.

"Hey," I said. "I tried some of Zowitzki's magic potion. I think I'm having side effects. Like death."

"You're having delusions. That supplement shit is harmless. And useless. It's just some low-rent rip-off. You want to gain weight? Stick with me." And he flicked a bag of cheese popcorn at my head. I tore it open and felt the normal world start to come back.

I LET MY EYES WANDER TO Lucy's blond mane in the middle of the flock of soccer girls who'd flopped onto the hillside, but she was barking at Madden, if a bark can have a purr to it, "*Yeah,* number fourteen!"

"Lefferts!" Ward shouted. "Get in there!" Madden called my number: the square in, which would take me right into Zowitzkiland. I caught the pass and braced for Zowitzki's blow. Instead, the linebacker let me off easy with a half shove.

"Zowitzki!" screamed Ward. "What kind of tackle was that?"

"My knee's sore, that's all," grumbled Zowitzki. "I don't want to mess it up more before Hesford."

"Yeah, well, next time I want to hear her scream."

I kept it zipped. For now. But on the next play, when I was supposed to just decoy Thorn, "she" laid a solid block at his legs, knocking him down, although it was Zowitzki I wanted a piece of. For his stupid supplements and my stupid paranoia and anyone else in his goon squad who had me in their sights.

"All *right,* Lefferts," growled Ward. First good thing he'd ever said.

Of course, three plays later, after the whistle on a running play, Thorn clocked me, helmet to helmet, throwing a forearm into my stomach for good measure. I hit the ground, rolled, hopped up, and shot him the finger.

For the next few minutes, there was sort of a shimmer at the edges of my field of vision. Concussion symptom. My first. Something like a badge of honor, I thought. But I wasn't about to tell Ward—or anyone—that I was in a different dimension. When the practice ended with two laps, my head was straight again. Martin and I led the pack, and we locked into a friendly sprint at the end. Eighty-five beat me by ten yards.

I'd just pulled off my helmet, and Will and I had started up the hill toward the locker room, when I heard a girl's voice—"Hiya, Jack"—in a singsongy tone. Lucy. Her legs were a mile long beneath her short soccer shorts.

"Hey," I said, looking around for Madden. But she was alone, walking up to the girls' locker room.

Martin shook his head. "Don't even think about it. Lucy's game is to try and keep Madden on a leash by testing new waters."

Martin kept walking. I waved at her. She waved back. I did some quick calculations. Do what any meathead would do and get lured by the Siren? Or do what *I* wanted to do: follow Martin's advice. Concentrate on Caroline.

"So I heard you had your visit with Zowitzki," Martin said in the locker room. "What are you going to do?"

"No way I do needles," I said, pulling off the jersey.

"Jack," he said, staring me in the face, with a very serious look. I guess this was going to be the final word from eighty-five. My last, best chance to keep him as the mentor. "Like I told you, it's all in your head. This game is mental. If you think you're good, you are. And you could be good. So don't . . . be . . . stupid."

"Then I'll be good," I said. And that was *me*, I think, actually meaning it.

I sat on my stool, savoring the ache of all the hits and the fact that I was still standing. Trying not to think of Lucy's legs . . . and picturing Caroline's shy smile.

"Hey, boss, good practice." It was Clune.

"You too," I said. "That counterplay? Who'd you block— the whole defensive line?"

He laughed a friendly laugh. "I love football, man," he said in his Boston accent. "Always have. Saturday mornings, my old man was always on the road. I'd go down to the school field and play with big kids, get my head bashed in, boy. But nothing ever felt as good as getting hit and hitting back."

"Where was your dad?" I said.

"On the road. Salesman. Army when I was a kid. I'll be the first guy in the family to go to college if I make it through here. Gotta get straight Bs, otherwise no college ball. Without Devin, I'd be dead."

"Devin? The thirds coach?"

"Yeah. He tutors me in science, on his own. For free. Good man. Mellow. Says he's gonna pull some strings for colleges. Then, the Big Man willing, I get an MBA and move the family up the North Shore. Outta Dorchester." He said it "Daw-ches-tah."

As soon as Clune headed for the showers, I walked over to the big guy's locker, leaned in, and picked up the jug of pills: 1,000-milligram vitamin C's. That was it. The kid had been telling the truth. He wasn't juiced. Not with that belly.

"So how's the running?" I said to Caroline at dinner.

"The woods are really beautiful—that's the problem." She smiled. "I'll be lucky if I don't get cut. I was on the trail where it goes through in the woods, and it was like I was gliding . . . you know how a deer kind of hops all over the place, but still gets where it's going? So, anyway . . . I kind of left the trail."

"You just took off? In the middle of practice? That's not the Callahan I know." She didn't seem to mind when I said it that way—as if I knew her. This was a good thing.

"I know, I know, but it was like being free. I even started just running uphill, and I found this old stone fireplace. The view was insane. So when I got back down, I told Booth I'd just gotten lost, even though the route is pretty obvious. Of course, she flipped." She laughed. "What was I thinking?"

"You weren't thinking," I said. "That's what sports are all about. Plus I have her in French, and she's schizoid."

"Tell me about it. So how's football?" she said.

I told her I made varsity. "Can you believe that?"

She slid over and bumped my shoulder with hers as she scraped at her peas. Which was a way of a girl maybe fist-bumping or something. To me, it was a lot more.

"Yeah," she said. "I can believe that."

I guess some guys remember touching a girl for the first time somewhere else. That shoulder felt pretty good to start with.

It was time to call home. I was feeling like maybe I'd finally gotten off the ground. Like I was dealing from strength for, well, maybe the first time ever. So the next morning before English, I used Josh's cell phone—like everyone except me, he'd given Ward an old one and kept his real one—and called my dad.

"Jack? Hey, boy. Good to hear from you. What's the news? How you settling in?"

I told him that it was going pretty good. How I'd lucked out on a roommate. But there were a few teachers who were more hard-ass than I'd figured on. Hearing his voice wasn't quite as weird as I'd thought it'd be. Maybe some wall had come down a little since he wasn't always in my face.

"Well, that's what they're there for. To set the limits for you, point you in the right directions. I know that it's hard for you to understand, but you're not really ready to make your own decisions yet."

Oh. Right. It was Dad. "I guess that's why I made the stupid decision to try out for football," I said.

"Yeah, how'd that work out?" he said, but I could tell he was looking at numbers on a computer screen.

"I made the team. The varsity."

There was a pause, and a silence. "Varsity? What position?"

"Third receiver. I'm a sub. Our first game is down in Concord Saturday, against Hesford, if you want to come."

Another pause. "Damn. I think I'm in Kansas City. The Royals are looking for a new stadium site, and we're in on the planning. I may have to become a Royals fan! Hey, wait a second. I have to take this."

I hung up.

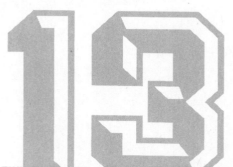

THE MUSIC ON THE KMART BOOM BOX WAS GERSHWIN. The three preludes. I'd tried to learn those a few years earlier. No dice.

Jarvis sat at his desk. This time the coffee mug said WE'RE WHEELING THRU WEST VIRGINIA! He gave back the *Gatsby* essays. He stopped at Caroline. "Some very deep observations here, but do you think it held together?"

Caroline shrugged. "I can't write essays."

Mine? A big red A, with no explanation. Weird.

Then he went to the whiteboard. "Okay. So who can tell me, what's the music?"

"Gershwin's preludes," I said.

Jarvis looked at me. "Jock Lefferts knows his tunes," he said.

"Hey, Jarvis was a little tough on you," I said to Caroline after we'd cleared the room.

"No, he was right. I'm not very good at writing. They tested me at my old school. Apparently I don't have any typical learning disabilities. I don't have ADHD, either of the 'inattentive' or 'hyperactive-impulsive' category," she said, punctuating the phrase with air quotes.

"Let's see. Oh, yeah. My 'proximal-distal planning' seemed to be within normal range. I also have no apparent 'executive function disorders' or 'visual processing disorders.' My 'phonological awareness' is normal, and therefore, in 'metacognitive' terms, there is no need for my teachers to consider 'remediating' me."

"That would mean drugs, right?"

"You got it. I dodged that one. Apparently I'm just having trouble coping with a 'high-stim' world that 'selects for multitasking.'"

I laughed. "How did you remember all of that?"

She smiled. "I don't know. I guess my memory isn't the problem. Then, I didn't even think there *was* a problem."

We'd reached the arts building "Maybe I just can't stay on the trail," she said. "See you." Then she peeled off into a practice room to join her octet. I headed past the frowning portraits, trying to sort through the stuff in my head. Like how her hair swung when she walked. Like how it felt as if she could be a great friend, if girls can be friends, and I didn't want to mess that up with any other feelings. But there were definitely some other feelings. Each time I saw her, even when she was off in the distance walking between classes, I'd started to try and see if she was walking with a guy. So far, so good.

• • •

I hadn't ever really had a girlfriend. Where I came from, unless people said your name in the hallways like you were some boldfaced guy, you didn't have much bait to fish with. Last summer, after everyone knew I was going on to prep school, I'd sort of been going out with a girl I'd met at a dance at some fancy hotel for people who went to prep schools. Everyone was dressed in tuxedos that didn't fit quite right and fake bow ties. She was drunk and pulled me out of a corner. She told me her last boyfriend was in college—a frat guy/hockey player from St. Lawrence who was majoring in prelaw. She went to Dalton, and she was pretty stuck up. I took her to some movies. I hadn't made any moves on her that first night, and the longer I waited, the harder it was to actually try.

Then one time when she'd been desperate to see *Kill Bill 2* again, in the middle of the movie she leaned over and said, "Tarantino is so, like, an *auteur*," and then suddenly her tongue was stabbing into my mouth so hard all I could think of was a snake. I tried to duel back with my own, but it was a losing war. It felt like we were jousting or something, which couldn't, I figured, be a positive thing. It was supposed to feel good, right?

She dropped me for a kid from Essex. Later Luke told me she'd told someone else she thought I was gay. Actually, I was just really relieved.

THE LESSON STARTED OUT OKAY. IT turned out that Hopper had the sheet music for the Gershwin preludes Jarvis had been playing in class, so we spent most of the lesson on the second one, where there was this part where you needed to be able to reach beyond an octave, and I could do it. It was one of the coolest pieces of music I'd ever heard. Definitely the greatest thing I'd ever tried to play.

"This is a good exercise, Jack." Hopper nodded, gazing out the window. "Five sharps. Good for the fingers. Like calisthenics on your football field. So. Have you come up with your audition piece?"

I hadn't given it a thought. So I said the first thing that came to mind. "Yessir, I think I have. These Gershwin preludes."

He turned slowly and shook his head at me. How was he going to get the professional cred he deserved if his students played "Three Blind Mice"?

"Jack, these are very simple pieces of music. Afterthoughts for a master. Challenging, but simple. And rather short. Anyone can play them, with a little practice."

"But I want to master them, sir," I said. "I really like play-ing them."

His face turned into stone. "Well, Jack," he said, "you'll have little chance of impressing me with an eight-minute set of preludes."

I wanted to say, "Like you impress me by coaching the contestants, and then being the judge. Kind of rigged, no?" But I kept it zipped as he stuffed his briefcase with papers and stomped out of the room.

I stuck around and played a bunch of angry measures that sounded like pissed-off crows at dawn. Jesus. Who was the adult, and who was the kid? Did *everyone* think I couldn't make any decisions for myself?

Our second receiver behind Will was a blond blazer kind of guy, a senior named Bannion, from a family that skied in Switzerland over spring break. He wasn't all that fast, and he didn't have great hands, but he could block, and the year be-fore, under Ward's run-heavy offensive scheme, he was good enough. He was our kicker, too, and he was so cocky that I figured he'd earned the spot just by acting like he deserved it, which was probably the way he'd live the rest of his life.

The next day in practice, Madden didn't throw me a single pass, even when the play was called for me. We spent most of the day practicing runs: Addison and Anthony kept trying to take it up our defense's gut, which was anchored by this huge nose tackle from Cleveland named Mancini. But he wasn't just huge, he was athletic. I didn't want anything to do with him. He reminded me of some bad guy in a Batman movie: he always had this lopsided smirky smile on his face after he made a tackle, and he liked doing these stupid dances whenever he planted Anthony into the ground.

After practice, Zowitzki walked up with EyeBlack streaming down his cheeks, like Marilyn Manson makeup gone mad. "So you on the program or not, chief?"

"Zowitzki," I said, "you ever look at the ingredients on that stuff?"

"Lefferts," he said, like he was talking to a little kid, "you know what's in a can of SpaghettiO's? That stuff'll kill you quicker than creatine will. Hey, if you want to skip the soft stuff and go straight to the top, just let me know. Like I said, they don't all need needles. But time's running out. If we start cycling you now, you'll be primed by the last few games. The beauty part, though, is that the attitude comes on a lot quicker than the abs. Juice gets wusses like you *mad,* you know? Why you think cops take 'em? No fear when the crackheads are comin' at 'em!"

"I'm not afraid," I said.

"You will be," he said, laughing an asshole laugh. "Hesford's gonna be easy on Saturday, but Chelton's after that, and they're dirty as crap. They clothesline, they hit you late, they lay the pain. They're fucking madmen!" He grinned. *"Literally."*

Then he laid a hand on my shoulder pad, all fake friendly. "Lefferts—it ain't just me wants you on the program. That guy with the golden arm has a say in this thing too, dude. Don't forget that he's the one throwing the passes to you. Or not throwing them."

The team bus was a high-end machine with tinted windows and a half dozen drop-down movie screens, showing the Adam Sandler remake of *The Longest Yard*. A couple of JV kids doing slave work were shoveling the equipment bags into the belly. I looked down, and the little quarterback, Alex, number 2, was waving up at me like a happy hobbit.

Bruno and Ward sat in the seat behind the driver, Ward with a clipboard, Bruno looking out the window. Madden and Addison sat in the other front seat. Zowitzki shared a seat right behind the quarterback, with Thorn. Clune took up a whole seat behind them, and Mancini a whole seat behind him. Most of the other players were watching the movie or listening to their iPods.

Martin was sitting alone halfway to the back, with his legs stretched across the empty seat next to him. He nodded, heavy-lidded, listening to his music. He lifted off the earphones. "Coltrane," he said, and put them back on.

I found an empty row near the back and sat down in the

window seat as the bus started to roll. "Hey," Anthony said, dropping down next to me. He had a copy of *Sports Illustrated*. "You think maybe we get some playing time today?" Now we pulled onto the road, and brown cornstalks started to roll by out the window. "Addison says we should kill them. They won, like, one game last year."

I tried to read *The Bacchae*, a play about the god of wine by an old guy named Euripedes, for history, but I couldn't concentrate. I wondered if I'd get a shot today. And if I did, could I pull this whole insane thing off?

A few minutes before we got to Hesford, Ward stood up in the middle of the bus and switched off the movie.

"All right: listen good. You know we're only playing six games this year because the little old ladies running the goddamned conference have decided that this sport is too dangerous for their precious little boys. So what's that mean for us, Addison?"

"Means we can't let a single one get away," Addison said.

"You got it. Listen to the Texan stud, boys. Heed those words. You look past these gals today, next thing you know, we're out of it—right out of the gate. So let's get it done, and let's get it done early. Don't look past 'em. Run right through 'em."

The Hesford campus was old and small. Their team was just as small, and slow, and didn't want any part of us. I stood on the sideline, half wanting in, half glad to be ignored. I wanted to contribute, but I also didn't want to mess up. So I spent a lot of time scanning the Hesford bleachers and the big lawn next to them on the home side, where parents sat surrounded by their dogs, watching their sons get whupped.

Out on the field, Addison was gaining about eight yards a carry, and Madden completed almost every pass he threw in the first half to Will and Bannion. Will caught two for TDs. Bruno didn't call a single pass play in the third quarter, showing a little mercy. I figured it was Bruno doing the calling because Ward would have wanted to score 117 points.

Anthony played a half dozen series, including a twenty-yard gain up the middle when he broke two tackles. On the sideline, I cheered him on and kept looking over at Ward, but I was nowhere on the radar until halfway through the fourth quarter, when he was suddenly next to me. "Next series, you're in for Bannion," he said, without looking at me. "Stay with your blocks. And don't screw up."

I slipped my helmet over my head, like I'd been doing for two weeks, but this time it took me three or four tries to buckle the chin strap. Bannion wandered over. We hadn't said a word to each other in the two weeks since I'd been on the team.

"The corner's pretty slow; block him low," he said, like he was maybe relieved he didn't have to play anymore.

I trotted into the huddle, leaned in to hear Madden's call. I was high, only it was a high I'd never felt. A real game. On a prep-school varsity team. Number 88. *Me.*

The play was a simple run for Anthony, to the left, over on Martin's side, so all I had to do was half block the corner. I thought about what it might feel like in a few months, playing at home, in the Essex game, with Caroline watching from the hillside.

I fired out at the cornerback, who looked at me like I was insane, because the play was way over on the other side. He backed off like a matador, and I fell down without him even touching me. Anthony had gotten a few yards. I heard Ward shout angrily, but when I looked over, it was Addison coming in to replace Anthony, not Bannion to replace me.

Madden called the next two plays to my side, with Addison running. I didn't exactly wipe out the cornerback, but I was so wired, I managed to tie him up enough for Addison to get some yardage. I was smacking him as much for me as for him. It felt good to make a statement with my body, even if it wasn't a very loud one. When the cornerback shouted to a ref, "Hey! He's holding!" I took it as a good sign. I was on the legal edge. I was playing football.

Now we were on the Hesford ten, knocking on the door again. Anthony ran in with the play from the sideline. There were just a few minutes left in the game, and I figured we'd run out the clock. But Anthony told Madden that Ward wanted a ten-yard square in—to me.

The call made no sense: totally piling on Hesford; it was already 31–7. But that was cool—the pressure was off, because we didn't need the score. All I thought was, *I can do this.* I lined up, looked over at the corner, then at the goal line, where I'd turn to catch the pass, and everything seemed crystal clear, almost floodlit. I was about to catch my first pass for Oakhurst Hall—for a touchdown no less.

I sprinted ten yards and hooked just as Madden fired the pass, but it wasn't anywhere *near* me; it was way too high, and worse, it was a few yards behind me. I reached back as the ball sailed way over my head. Then I relaxed, figuring the play was over. And that's when the cornerback I'd been blocking all day hit me full speed with his helmet in the back of my shoulder, like a battering ram.

I hit the ground. For a second, I couldn't breathe, but I'd be damned if I was going to lie there like some beached fish. I got up and staggered in a circle.

Time had run out. The team huddled, cheering each other, slapping pads. I was on the outside of the cluster, leaning in, as the chant of "*OAK*-hurst *HA*-all" rose from the pack. Then the coaches gathered us at the end of the field, underneath the goalposts.

Bruno stood with his arms folded and slowly scanned the team. "Good win, men." It was the first time I'd heard his voice at full volume. "Good concentration. Good start. Be proud." Then he moved away, and Ward took over.

"But we should have shut them out," he said. "If we play like this against Chelton on Saturday, you're going to embarrass the whole school. I want more dedication, better blocks, better tackles. But hey, we got the W, and that's what it's all about. Hit the bus."

"That was bullshit, man," Anthony said, flopping down beside me. "Cheap hit."

"Not as bullshit as Madden throwing it behind me," I said.

"You think he did it on purpose? No way. Everyone throws a bad pass sometimes. He may be a jerk, but I don't think he's an asshole."

"What's the difference?"

"Zowitzki's an asshole," Anthony explained. "Madden? I don't think anyone ever told him he wasn't a stud. High-school star in Ohio. Got here with his arm. So he acts like one. But there's gotta be a normal guy in there somewhere. He just hasn't had to be one yet."

The sermon was Ecclesiastes: "To every thing, there is a season," Carlton chanted from his wooden cherry picker. "Like the seasons, you will always return to the lessons you've learned here. And many of you will return to this campus many times over your adult lifetimes. Turn, turn, turn."

"Great song by the Byrds," Sam whispered.

It seemed like just another stupid sermon—until Carlton dropped the bomb. "But speaking of the campus, I have noticed a very disturbing trend lately: you are all strolling our beautiful grounds with earplugs plugged in your ears, listening to what could be called music, by some, while ignoring God's beauty all around you. You are longer speaking to each other. No longer exchanging ideas. It has disturbed me to see this student body become so antisocial, and I am prepared to do something drastic. I am prepared to confiscate your iPods should I see this alarming trend continue." A collective groan spread through the chapel—the first sign I'd seen that there was a soul inside Oakhurst Hall's walls. Carlton ignored it. "It hardly strikes a scholarly image to visiting parents if they can't see students engaged in debate and discussion on our spacious campus."

What was funny was that he was talking about people listening, and by now, no one was listening to him.

"Notice that he didn't say 'prospective students,'" Sam said, as we walked up the path. "Dude knows where the honey flows from."

"Hey, how come you know more about our music and movies than I do?"

"We have to know everything about everything," he said, deadpan as usual. "That's our secret assignment. They send us here to spy on your country, then we take everything we've learned back home and try to get it right. As opposed to what you guys do, which is mess everything up. Ever notice how none of you are smiling around this place? Unless you're high? And we smile? And none of us get high? It's all a game. Like the man said, 'No matter where you go, there you are.'"

I tried to figure that one out. Then I got it: Wherever you are, that's where you are, so you had to deal with it. "Buddha?"

"Peter Weller. *The Adventures of Buckaroo Banzai Across the Eighth Dimension.* I can't believe you don't know any of this stuff."

The pretty Korean girl from English joined us. Sam introduced her as Seo Woon Bae. "Sang-Ook's told me a lot about you," she said.

"All bad, I hope," I said.

Seo Woon stopped in her tracks and looked me straight in the eye. "Yes, I'm afraid. All of it. I'm so sorry. He really does not like you, not at all. But he's too polite to say so."

Then they walked on ahead, holding hands.

I wanted their lives.

I found a bench-press place in a far corner, away from the half dozen other kids—a few linemen, Anthony—and away from the mirrors. No music was blasting, just the rhythmic clank of Anthony's reps on the Universal across the room, which made a melody start to noodle in my head.

It was moody and waterfall-y. Sometimes music wrote itself.

Within a couple of minutes, the knot in my back was gone, and when I was done—thirty reps at sixty pounds—I waited for my muscles to complain, but they didn't. I was getting in football shape.

I had just walked out of the gym on a definite—and natural—endorphin high when I saw Jarvis walking across the quad, head down, piles of books cradled under one arm. He looked up, preoccupied. "Hey, Jock," he said, smiling, not slowing down, so I hurried to fall in with him. There was something about Jarvis that felt like it was worth following. "How's football going?" he said.

"I could do without some of the kids who play it," I said. "They're not exactly my type. Whatever that is."

Jarvis laughed, a little nervously. Jarvis did everything nervously. "Everyone fits in somewhere. Some of us have to look a little harder to find where, is all. So you enjoying the class?"

"Yeah, I really am. I'm not sure I get everything, though."

"Well, if you don't understand something, for God's sake, ask someone who does. Just not me," he said, and walked away down the long entrance drive.

The carillon bells rang, signaling the hour—the cheery *B-G-A-D, D-A-B-G* which always sounded so hopeful—until the drone: *dong, dong, dong* . . . twelve minor notes that didn't even sound like musical notes. By the end, it felt like getting hit over the head with a rubber mallet.

Carlton music.

"THE BACCHAE," BRUNO SAID. **"WHY DOES** it speak to us, two millennia later?"

Thorn's hand shot in the air. "Sir, it isn't speaking to me." He had acne on his back and a jaw that seemed a little too square. I'd done some research. 'Roids.

"No, Thorn," Bruno said, grabbing a stack of graded papers, "because, as usual, you're just not listening." The alpha girls giggled. "Good job on the al-Qaeda papers, people. But in the future, Miss Bae, I'd prefer that you didn't use big-budget Hollywood movies in your bibliography."

"Aw, come on, Mister B," said Seo Woon, "*300* was an awesome movie, admit it."

"Good special effects—I'll give you that," he said, with the slightest of smiles, and the class laughed. "But in the end, who won?"

Lucy's pink fingernails shot into the air. "The Persians won that battle, but the Greek navy turned them back at Salamis, which was the battle that counted. I guess that's what they mean when they say you have to pick your battles to win your war."

"Good. All of you should keep that in mind," Bruno said, scanning the room. "It doesn't just apply to war."

Why was he looking at me?

"I saw this *Rocky & Bullwinkle*," said Seo Woon, "where they go back and end up in this war with swords, only if it's Sparta, it should have been spears, right, Mr. Bruno?"

"The weapons change. Nothing else does," says Bruno.

"Sparta back then, Oakhurst now," I said. I think it was the second thing I'd ever said in history. "Our football team is bigger than their hoplites ever were."

This got the second half smile of the day out of Bruno.

"Hiya, Jackster," Lucy said, catching up with me after class.

Jackster?

I was on my way to the gym during a free period, even though I should have been doing homework. In a weird way, weights had become one of my favorite things to do, at least when the weight room was empty during classes. It was something I could get better at, every day. And I never got worse. It was like laying bricks that were becoming a wall.

"What's up?" I tried to sound cool. She was wearing a tight black skirt and a pink shirt and a black sweater. A black head-band shoved her blond hair straight back. Catalogue sexy.

"Nothing much," she said.

I flashed on what Will had said about her games.

Then another Muffy caught up to us. She looked over at

me like some bug she'd just found squashed on the heel of her shoe. "Luce—you *have* to see what Melanie's done with her room. It's insane."

"Just a sec," said Lucy. The girl shot me a glare and walked away.

"So," Lucy said to me, "where you going now? I've got a free period."

"Gym," I said. "Gotta get some lifting in. You know. We play Chelton Saturday."

Lauy rolled her eyes. "God," she said. "Doesn't anything count around here except *football*?"

"Music counts," I said. "I'm in a cool band."

"Well, I'm glad to hear you're so busy," she said. "So maybe we could actually hang out together, if you ever have the *time*." Then she walked double-speed up the path, like a thoroughbred horse.

At Jarvis's table, kids reached for whatever they wanted, and came and went whenever they felt like it. He cut off anyone bitching and moaning, but other than that, anything was fair game to talk about. At one dinner, we had our "academic adviser" chat—as in, "You failing anything? No? Good. Pass the fries." It was like what I always thought a big Italian family table would be like.

A boringly pretty girl from San Francisco had replaced Caroline to my right. Her hair was short and stylish. The first night I asked her what she was interested in, and she said "St. Bart's." She asked me what I was interested in, and I said music.

"I *love* Jay-Z," she said. "Who do you listen to?"

"Me? I don't know—Elbow, the Thrills. Some vintage Wall of Voodoo. You know . . . the usual." She smiled with her mouth. The rest of her didn't move. She turned to the kid next to her on the other side. His hair was perfect.

On my left, Spencer was gone too, but this time I'd traded up. He'd been replaced by Alex, the little quarterback. I asked about the team. He answered the way he'd always talked: real fast. "The starting quarterback is a jerk, and his roommate's father is like in the cabinet or something like with the president—like, that cabinet—and so the quarterback's roomie said to me yesterday, 'We can beat you in a game of touch anytime with any other player: twenty bucks a man.' So I was thinking that maybe you could be the receiver for me if you wanted, because we could play them two-on-two and pick up twenty bucks, because the quarterback's arm is good, but you could probably cover the rich kid easy, and I could really use twenty bucks because my parents always say they're putting money into my account, but they never do on time, because they can't even pay the tuition on time."

By now, I was laughing out loud. Alex was like some puppy that could talk.

"And if we lose, can you cover your half?"

"We won't lose," he said, and he wasn't smiling when he said it.

I flashed back to the day I got here, when I caught that weird pass. I kind of wanted that feeling back.

"I'm in," I said.

The rules were this, down on a gusty little thirds soccer field surrounded on three sides by woods: You had to score a TD on four downs, or the ball went over to the other guys and they got four shots. Winner was the first to score four.

The rich roommate wore a long-sleeved T-shirt with the name of a yacht club on it, Princeton sweats, and running shoes that no white kid should be wearing unless he had a million-dollar hip-hop deal.

On the first series, I covered him, and he threw a good fake. I fell for it, and worse, I fell down. I'd never played defense. The kid pulled the pass in, and just like that, the other guys were up 1–0. I was pissed at myself.

"Sorry," I said to Alex. "Won't happen again."

"My guess is you just saw his one move," Alex said, all business now, what with bucks on the line. "He's not that fast, and he has a pigeon brain. No learning curve. Okay, our turn. Just blow by him."

I didn't even have to throw a fake. He couldn't keep up with me. Alex's pass was perfect. I caught it in stride, loped past the soccer goal, and from then on in, it was easy. I used different patterns: down-and-in, comeback, comeback-fake-then-long. Alex's passes were nearly all perfect. If he'd been a foot taller, he'd have been getting Big Ten offers already.

And he was right: yacht boy had one move on offense and not enough speed to back it up. And if I also did a little grabbing of his stupid yacht club shirt, sue me.

Candy from a baby.

"Good game, guys," the rich kid said, peeling off two twenties: the kid was only in it for the action. Money meant nothing to him. Except to play with it. Gambling was Yacht Kid's high. "Next week? Same time? Same place? I got your routes down now, Lefferts," he said, smiling, looking me in the eye. Then he shook my hand, like I guess yachtsmen do. I almost felt bad knowing that I'd be taking his money. Almost.

"You got it," Alex said.

They walked off ahead of us. The QB was ranting at Yacht Boy.

Alex kissed his twenty, put it in his pocket. "What are you going to spend yours on?" he asked.

"Calculus," I answered.

Spencer looked only mildly surprised when he answered the door in his dorm, a new building way out on the fringe of the campus. "Hey," he said, turning around and sort of welcoming me into his room. It had posters of guys I'd never heard of. Black-and-white. I guessed they were scientists who'd figured stuff out that had to be figured out. But Eddie Vedder's scratchy warble rattled the window; I hadn't figured him for a Pearl Jam guy.

"What's up?" he said.

"I just thought I'd come by, see how you're doing," I said. "Hey, how do you rate a single?"

"The kids they can't figure out, they put 'em into this place. They're all singles in Farnstead."

I scanned his desk: three laptops, all connected. My guess was he was hacking NASA. "So," I said, pulling the bill out of my pocket, "you got a minute?"

A half hour later, I not only knew what sines, cosines, and tangents were, I knew about cusps and antipodes, which until then I would have said were things you'd see in a river.

"Same time, next week?" I said.

"Sure," he said, bent over a MacBook Air he'd pulled out of a purple case, already happily adrift somewhere in a parallel universe. "This is unbelievable," he said out loud to himself. "First, life might survive on Europa. Now they found new bacteria under Lake Vostok! A kind of life no one's ever seen on Earth!"

I slipped into the hall and ran into Simon coming up the stairs with a book bag. He invited me into his room. On one wall was a poster of a bunch of lakes in England. A few magazines I'd never seen were scattered next to a futon. *Forest* magazine. *Arizona Highways.* I flopped down on his floor, and picked up *Desert Illustrated*. It was from 1949. "What's this?"

He shrugged. "I meditate on the mountain every day. That wine god in *The Bacchae* has it right: nature against civilization, nature always wins. You start your paper yet?"

"I don't even understand what's going on in the stupid play," I admitted.

"Basically, the god of wine and drugs comes to town to get revenge on the king who dissed his mother. His worshipers all trip on bliss in the woods and kill the king, and then the king's mother comes down from her trip and realizes she's holding her own kid's head. The city falls apart."

I thought of Caroline and her runs in the woods.

"Nature rules. If someone's acting 'naturally,' it's a good thing, right? You know, 'follow your nature.'"

"I can't stand it when people ask me what I want to be," I said. "Like I'm supposed to have an idea."

"But you *are* someone already, dude. We *all* are. Well, except for the blazers and the Muffys and the scenesters. That's what's so fucked up about this place. The adults all think we're unformed adults, like apprentice grown-ups. But we're our own tribe, with our own shit to deal with. Why else would we do all the weird escapist stuf we do? Why else do so many of us kill ourselves? Get high? Get laid? Because we have our own radar, and our own world, and it's not *behind* theirs . . . it's *ahead*. Come on—think of the last time when you were feeling really, really good—not high, just, you know: riffing, listening to a band, kissing a babe?"

Looking at the swaying of Caroline's hair. Smelling how clean she always smelled.

"So now when was the last time you thought some grown-up felt that way? Ever? They have it backwards, man. All adults are is shriveled, over-the-hill teenagers."

Our own tribe. I liked the sound of it. I was a member of something.

THE NEXT DAY IN PRACTICE, I took the place of Bannion, the other receiver, for the second series. On the first running play, Thorn crack-backed with a dirty block on my knees. A sharp pain knifed up my thigh. I jumped up in the kid's face. "What the hell was that about?"

He sneered from behind his face guard. "Suck it up, Lefferts. You ain't seen nothin' yet."

Now Madden called a buttonhook to me, but before we broke the huddle, Will said, "Hey, Vic, maybe you can throw it somewhere Lefferts won't get killed?"

Everybody froze. "I don't know what you're talking about, Martin," said Madden.

The rest of the offense exchanged glances. Clune broke up the freeze when he barked, "Okay, let's just play some fucking football."

I ran my pattern, pivoting on a dime. The ball was exactly where it was supposed to be. I pulled it in for an easy eight yards and turned upfield just as Ward blew his whistle to end the play. Then Zowitzki hit me low, at the knees. And Thorn hit me high, a helmet-to-helmet spear.

The ball went flying into the air. Zowitzki pounced on it, popped to his feet and spiked it. Then he and Thorn high-fived.

"One more fumble, Lefferts," Ward said, "and you're back down on the pond."

And that was enough.

"The play was over!" I shouted. "You blew the god-damned whistle!"

The team was quiet. I glanced around at the faces and stopped when I saw Bruno looking at me with the usual stone face. The look felt like a green light.

Ward stared at me. "You challenging me, son?"

"I'm challenging the rules of your practices, sir," I said. "They're getting me killed. If you want me to catch passes, I can't do it if I'm dead. If you want to get me killed, don't bother. Just send me down to the pond."

We stared each other down. Everyone else just sort of looked everywhere else. Then Bruno turned around and slowly walked in the other direction. Ward didn't say anything. I had a weird feeling that I'd gained some ground. But Madden didn't throw me another pass the rest of the practice. He didn't throw one to Martin, either. Bannion was suddenly his favorite receiver.

After practice, Ward called me over. If the man wanted a showdown, I was *so* ready. But instead, he acted like nothing had ever happened. "A heads-up, Lefferts," he said, eyes glued to his clipboard. "You're in the game plan for tomorrow against Chelton. Be ready."

Like I wasn't always ready? "Cool," I said, and walked away.

Score one for being yourself.

In the locker room, I asked Clune why Ward said I'd be part of the game plan.

"Chelton's a football factory for second-chance kids," he said. "So they probably paid some Hesford coach to fill them in on our personnel. You weren't on the highlight reel. So maybe he figures it'll mess them up if you're part of the game." He popped some of his horse vitamins. "Or maybe he figures they'll break your leg, and he won't have to worry about you anymore."

"Thanks, Clune."

"Anytime."

All over campus Audis and Lexuses and Suburbans were parked nose to tail, on curbs, on paths. The stands and the hillside were packed. I looked through the sea of faces and prep clothes for Caroline, but all I saw was Carlton, dead center on the hillside, on a blue Oakhurst Hall blanket, sitting next to McGregor, the lacrosse-tie admissions guy.

As game time neared, linemen were smacking each others' shoulder pads. Zowitzki and Thorn were actually punching each other in the stomach. I guess to make them even tougher. Madden was whipping passes to Bannion.

And Will was sitting at the end of the bench with a thousand-yard stare in his eyes.

Bruno called us in for a huddle before the kickoff. "Good luck, men—and give it your all," was all he said. Then slapped my helmet as he walked away. Not real hard. Friendly.

Pick your battles to win your wars, right? Maybe I'd picked a good time for my first battle in practice the day before.

But then, I still didn't know if it was Bruno who actually ran the team or Ward, who, of course, was hyped like a maniac.

"This is it!" he shouted. "This is the real thing!" he ranted. "There's a lot of people on that hillside counting on you. Don't let the Hall down!"

Hell, even I got caught up in the rush. But I was relieved that they kept me out for the first quarter, when neither team scored. The hits were a lot louder than last week. Most of them came from Zowitzki. In the first quarter, he made four solo tackles. He was like the Tasmanian Devil in those old cartoons—bouncing off blockers and slamming Chelton runners to the ground, including one kid who had to be helped off the field. Every tackle brought roars from the hill.

Ward—Bruno?—sent me in to start the second quarter. On the first play, Madden called a pass for me: a break to the sideline. This was it. This was time to prove I could do this, in front of everyone. Was she watching?

I ran the pattern perfectly. When I got close to their guy, I looked left, to fake him, and cut sharp to the outside . . . but when I tried to pivot, it was as if I was suddenly running in place, like in a dream. The cornerback had hooked his fingers into my pants. Madden had to throw the ball away.

"Lefferts, get your ass open!" he said in the huddle.

"He was holding my belt!"

"No shit, Sherlock," grumbled Clune. "They're dirty. Dirty 'em back."

We had to punt. Back on the sideline, Will sidled over. "Slap his arms away before he can get his hands on you." He did some karate-like thing, bringing his hands up together, then shooting them out. "They won't call it."

For the rest of the quarter, Addison kept pounding the middle, but he was getting nowhere. Chelton had a huge nose tackle who was shouting out the defensive formation with a weird accent. Like Russian. A prep school recruit from Russia? Clune had been right: prep football didn't have many rules.

Our only long play was a slant across the middle to Will, who broke it for twenty-five. But it was called back because Bannion had lined up offside. So Ward put me in for one more series before the half.

We were driving. On a first down in Chelton's territory,

Madden called another square out. I slapped the cornerback's arms away with my new martial-arts skills, broke right, and I was looking it into my hands—until the cornerback, playing me like Velcro, reached over my shoulder and broke it up.

As I walked back to the huddle, I heard Ward yell, "JEE-sus, Lefferts! Get separation!"

Which I ignored.

I knew I'd fucked up. I didn't need a loser to tell me I was a loser.

It was scoreless at the half.

"These guys ain't Hesford," Anthony said as we walked over to gather beneath the goalposts for the halftime talk.

This interlude wasn't going to be pretty.

Bruno stood to the side, head bent over a notebook. He could have been looking at notes on Sparta's hoplites for all the expression on his face. Ward looked at us in disgust, as if we'd played so badly we didn't even deserve to be ripped. As if Chelton weren't a semipro team that pretended it was a prep school.

He shook his head. Then all he said was, "Go ahead. Let your parents down." And drifted over to Bruno.

A few seconds later, Zowitzki broke the silence, loud enough to be heard by every tweedy alum up on the hillside: *"FUCK THIS!"*

He was out of control. He was red-faced. He was breathing hard and fast. Then he brought it down to a whisper. "I will not lose to these freaks because you assholes on offense can't get your shit together." Then he turned around and walked away.

Then Clune walked to the place where Zowitzki had been and looked at the ground. He was bouncing his helmet off his thigh pad. I thought I saw blood on his pants. The guy was playing his ass off. Then he looked up.

"It's pretty simple, guys," he said. "You gonna get beat by losers? Or you gonna play smart? This is Oakhurst Hall, man. Start playing like it means something!" Then he took the helmet, raised it up, and planted it on his head. We all did the same thing and followed him to the sideline.

The second half began like the first: no scoring, and big hits. Then, halfway through the fourth quarter, Zowitzki blocked a Chelton punt, picked it up, and ran it deep into Chelton territory.

And . . . Bruno sent me in with Anthony. On first down, Anthony ran a sweep behind me. I lowered myself and tried to lay a block on the cornerback, but the kid had size and momentum, and he bowled me over. The kid nailed Anthony—and the ball popped loose, bouncing crazily up the field, followed by a bunch of Chelton kids.

The thought hit me in a microsecond: I hadn't just messed up . . . I'd allowed a fumble! But then, no more thoughts: time to act.

I bounced up, raced toward the ball, and pounced on it

at the same time as a Chelton kid. Now we were both grabbing at it. But for me, something primal was taking over.
Trying to capture the football, I was suddenly fighting out
at everyone who thought I couldn't do it. I was throwing my
elbows, and I might have even bitten the dude's arm. I just
ripped the sucker out of his hands, and when bodies started
landing on top of me, I held on to it even harder. No one was
going to get this football.

At the bottom of the pile, I felt one hand grab for my
balls and another scratch my forehead, trying to peel my
helmet off backward. And my head with it.

But when the refs pulled the pile away, I still had the ball.

We'd actually gained ten yards.

"Shitty block. Nice recovery," said Clune back in the
huddle. "Also, you're bleeding."

I reached up to my forehead, felt blood. Licked it off my
fingertip. I liked the coppery taste. *Football.*

Maybe Madden knew I'd be pissed. He called the same
play, and this time, I tied up the cornerback and Anthony
bounced off a linebacker and got twelve, and a first down.

Anthony and I came out. On the next three plays, Addison plowed up the middle for good gains. We were down to
Chelton's eight-yard line.

"Lefferts!" Ward shouted to me. "Get in there. Tell Madden
to call an RV-80."

I had no idea what an RV-80 was. Madden looked at me,

nodded to the huddle. "Reverse to Lefferts. Martin, take out that linebacker. Addison, you got the cornerback."

A reverse? We'd never practiced a reverse.

"Break back, come around behind Madden going the other way," Will told me, as we went to the line. "You take the handoff. Just follow me."

It was time to turn on some speed. On the snap, I took one step forward to freeze the cornerback, then turned around and ran back to Madden, who turned to hand the ball off to me.

But just as I got ready to take the ball, he pulled it back in to his stomach.

I kept running a few yards, empty-handed, and looked back to see Madden run straight up the middle into the end zone, untouched. Touchdown.

I heard the hillside erupt in cheers as a Chelton linebacker laid me out with a clean hit, shoulder pad to helmet. Pissed-off payback. Then he kneed me in the ribs as he climbed off.

I got up just in time to see the team mobbing Madden.

On the sideline, Will gave me a friendly slap on the helmet. "That *so* had to be planned. A Bruno special. Madden was never going to hand it off to you, but only Madden and Bruno knew that. The perfect fake. We all blocked it like you were going to get it, and Chelton followed us. That's what they got Bruno for, I guess. He sure as hell knows how to call a play."

Bannion kicked the extra point, and in this game, no one was going to get any more points. They'd be lucky to get out alive. There were two fights in the fourth quarter, and Zowitzki was limping. But we won, 7–0. At the final gun, while the team celebrated, I was standing on the outside of the victory huddle when Anthony gave me a high five. "Thanks for saving my ass on that fumble. And nice fake on the reverse."

"It wasn't a fake," I said. "I thought I was going to get the ball."

So that's what Ward meant about me being in the game plan. Great. I was the varsity decoy.

Still, when I walked up the hill, parents I didn't even know reached to slap me on my pads. Not mine, but parents anyway. And I had some blood to show for it.

A half hour later, Caroline was there to meet me coming out of the gym. "That didn't look like a lot of fun," she said. "I mean that fumble."

"Yeah, well. I guess it's part of the game," I said. As if I was some pro.

"You're going to need another bandage on that," she said, as we walked toward the quad, and pointed to my forehead. "Well, I guess if there's something you want, and you want it badly enough, it's going to be painful to get it sometimes, right?"

"I guess," I said. I was hoping she might want to change the bandage herself, but she walked me to the library, where she paused, then closed her eyes and said, "'The thing about life is that you must survive. Life is going to be difficult, and dreadful things will happen. What you do is move along, get on with it, and be tough. Not in the sense of being mean to others, but being tough with yourself and making a deadly effort not to be defeated.'"

"Let me guess," I said. *"Gatsby."*

"Nope, Katharine Hepburn. My hero. Did you know she had a fire going in her fireplace in Connecticut every day of the year? That's my idea of hearth and home. See you later."

Mine too, as of, like, now.

THAT NIGHT, JOSH GOT A TEXT. "Guerrilla rehearsal," he said. "The boys want to play." Sounded just right. I was more than ready for some music.

In the practice room, Josh pulled a pint of Jack Daniel's out of his guitar case. Danny cut the lights. The red of the exit sign and the red blinks on the amps glowed.

They passed the bottle around. When it got to me, I figured we'd be screwed if we were caught, but the weird way the game went down, and Hopper's ghost hovering somewhere in this goddamned perfect building—it all added up enough to push me just far enough. Or too far. I took one long swallow of the whiskey. It burned its way down my throat. Then it hit the back of my head.

I handed the bottle back to Josh, who took a long gulp and gave it back to me. I didn't want any more. But right then, I didn't care. I wanted to be part of the team. I took another hit. Then I handed it to Danny.

Josh picked up his guitar and played his four-note birdsong, softly, then stopped. "Naw," he said. "Not tonight. Let's rock." He buzz-sawed a single, screaming chord. Simon answered with two hard slams on his tom-tom.

Then my hands kind of leapt to the keyboard. I slammed a bunch of heavy, predictable rock chords with my left hand. Meantime, through the whiskey, without my brain even trying, my right hand needled out a decent, rambling solo. Somewhere in there was an echo of the Schubert from a few days ago. Mostly, I was playing too hard: pissed-off piano. But it wasn't all that bad.

I finished the solo and looked over at Danny. He nodded once and launched into a hard-rock riff. Then he repeated it. Then I repeated it, kind of. Then Josh repeated it. Kind of. And for the next five minutes, we pounded out some crazy, hard, pure-rock progression, sloppy as hell. Early Nine Inch Nails meets Nirvana.

Simon knew how to finish it off: with a final, heavy, slam-drum thing.

We just stood there, each echoing it in a different way in our heads.

"That's kind of cool," Josh said.

"Kind of, I don't know, like . . ." Danny said.

"A mess," I heard the whiskey say. Speaking for me.

Josh looked away. Simon laughed.

But Danny didn't. "I thought it *ruled,* man," he said.

"It could be the middle movement of our little rock symphony if we cleaned it. What'd you call it? The Rapids?"

"It was all over the place," I said. This time it was me *and*
the booze talking. "And I'll bet you fifty bucks we can't do
it again. And if all we're going to do is get wasted, then it's
not music."

I could tell that all of them wanted to answer, but none
of them did. Maybe, just maybe, I'd struck a chord. So I kept
going. "I don't know about you guys, but I think we have
sort of a real good vibe here," I said. "You're all better than
anyone I've ever played with. Which is why I want to take it
somewhere beyond slack-rock bullshit."

Suddenly, the lights went on in the hallway.

"Shit!" said Simon, sticking the bottle inside his bass drum.

"Cool out," Josh said. He opened the door a crack and
came back. "No prob. Just Mario."

"Geek," said Danny.

"Serious about his music," I said.

They all started packing up. Maybe I'd gone too far. I
walked out by myself. Then Josh caught up, carrying his guitar.

"Kinda harsh," he said.

"Maybe," I said.

"Not that, like, it doesn't make sense," he said.

"We could do some serious stuff here," I said. "But we
have to take it seriously."

Josh stopped, and I stopped, and he looked at me in

a new way: not as my stoner roommate, but as a kid with a brain, facing off with me.

"Dude, check it out," he said. "Everything about this place is too goddamned serious. I do the band to cool out."

I didn't answer for a second. Took a breath. It was put-up or shut-up time. "That's why *we* have to take it seriously," I said. "If we're just some carnival act, nothing will ever change around this place. But if we convince old Oak that the classical scene isn't the only way to play the game, maybe we can be a little more visible."

He laughed. "Since when does music matter to the Master Race?"

"Because," I said, "we don't make music; music makes *us*."

He smiled. "Where'd you get that?"

I had no idea. The whiskey? It had just appeared in my brain. A Jack Lefferts original thought! Even if it was a little hokey.

"Okay," Josh said. "No more of the amber liquids at practice."

"Or weed."

"Ouch," he said.

When I woke up the next morning, I was sore in every corner of my body. Including my brain.

"Rough night?" Sam said as we took our usual route up the shrub-lined path after a sermon about something or other. I hadn't heard a word. But the final hymn was cool.

"Rough day, then rough night," I said. "Chelton's line weighed six thousand pounds. I was under it. Then I had a few drinks with the band. Which is not going to happen again."

"Which is why Koreans don't play football," Sam said. "We stick to the noncontact sports. We'll be the last ones standing. *We will . . . survive*," he sang.

"Don't tell me," I said. "Metallica?"

He rolled his eyes. "Grateful Dead. 'Touch of Grey.' Jesus, Jack. Didn't you ever take history?"

In the weight room, my shoulder throbbed as I did my first reps on the Universal. The clanks were too loud. I closed my eyes, started pumping again, and stopped. Something in the back of my neck clicked every time I looked to my right. My left wrist hurt. Even playing the piano was going to hurt.

"Feeling the pain?" It was Zowitzki, standing over me, lifting a ten-pound barbell with each arm, first left, then right, like a piston engine, huffing in rhythm. "The offer still stands."

"I don't need to get big, Zowitzki," I said. "I need to get open. I don't need your miracle drugs."

"Nothing miraculous about 'em," Zowitzki said. "Just

science. Anabolics make the recovery time quicker too. Trust me. It's quick and painless."

"Okay, so I've been wondering," I said. "Where exactly does the needle go?"

"In your butt."

I had to laugh. The macho men? Shooting up in each others' butts? Somehow I kept myself from saying something stupid enough to have him punch me out.

"It's only going to get worse for you," Zowitzki said, sitting down on the next bench. "The hurt just piles up during the season."

"So basically you're telling me to take a drug so I can recover from injuries I'm getting from my own team."

"Don't be paranoid, Lefferts," said the linebacker, walking away.

I went back to the weights. This time I ignored the hurt. Each time I pumped a weight, it was a slap back at Zowitzki.

"Why don't you call it a day?" Mr. Jarvis said, dropping down onto the next bench, in workout clothes, with a towel around his neck. "Let's get out of here."

He was a welcome sight. I liked Jarvis. He wore the tweed, but something about his smile made it seem like he knew it was just a costume. If someone's eyes could be, well, *kind,* his were. Whatever he wanted to talk about, it wasn't going to be bad.

We broke into the cool October air and walked down to the hillside overlooking the field. When he sat down, I followed. "Coulda used you Saturday," he said. The JVs had been stomped by Chelton.

"I wish you were up here," I said. "Ward's insane, Mr. Jarvis."

He laughed. "No, just insecure and taking it out on kids. It's the only world he knows. It's his safe place, as they say. We all need one."

I was looking over at the hill behind the field, the woods where Caroline ran cross-country. Neither of us said anything. I had this weird feeling that Jarvis had actually asked me to sit down on the hallowed hillside just to shoot the shit with someone. Josh had given me his bio: from the Bronx, went to Essex for a while on a soccer scholarship, dropped out of our biggest rival because he was working class and Essex had no class, just an endowment that could buy the Chrysler Building for a party favor at an alumni reunion.

"So how'd you end up teaching here, sir?"

"I needed a job," he said. "Got a full ride at Colgate for soccer, blew out a knee, studied journalism, bounced around some bad newspapers, didn't have the guts to go for the great American novel. They had an English spot down here: free food, free housing. Eighteen years later, I'm still on the treadmill."

"But you're really smart, and you're a really good teacher. Why aren't you teaching college or something?"

He flopped onto his back and put his hands behind his head.

"Maybe I think I'm needed here, or maybe I'm kidding myself, and I just don't have the chops for Dartmouth. But I know the ropes. I know what it's like to be at one of these places. I mean, what kid wants his parents to drop him off in a castle in the woods at a time in his life when the kid needs his folks more than ever?" He plucked a piece of grass and started to chew on it. "I guess I stick around," he said, "because trying to help kids figure it all out is what I'm good at."

It was like he was talking to himself.

"Mr. Jarvis, why do people send their kids to prep schools?"

"Well," he said, "there's a couple of centuries of history that say that sending your kid away into the world is how to make him a man."

"But this isn't the world," I said.

"Yeah, but trust me . . . the world's not much of a picnic, either." Then, in about a half second, he was back in focus and looking over at me. "So, Jack—you have some sort of gift with those hands, okay? I was watching a practice the other day, and"—he lapsed into a mock-comic McGregor voice—"as your adviser speaking, son,"—then he went back to his own voice—"you have the athlete gene. I had it too.

Sometimes it can be a curse. I wish I had a buck for every old Essex or Colgate guy who lives off memories of scoring some meaningless goal.

"But you have something else going on in your head. I don't think you'll ever lock onto old Oakhurst Hall as the glory days of your life. So forget Ward. He's a puppet. Carlton didn't hire Bruno just for his resume. You heard about Bruno's background, right? You probably don't know that he also paid the whole college rides of the three brothers and sisters in the family of that kid he slugged back in the day. He made a mistake. He flipped one time. Everyone does. Now the guy's at peace. And he thinks fairly highly of you."

I thought of telling Jarvis about the juicers. I wondered if Bruno knew. But something stopped me. The team was fucked up, but it was *my* team. It had to stay in the family. "But why does he let Ward ride me? Why's half the defense all over me? What's their problem?"

"You like the game?"

"I love it," I said.

"Then stop worrying about everyone else trying to turn you into something you're not, Jack. Play *your* game."

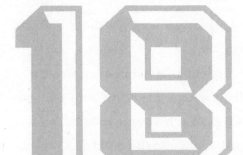

I FOUND THIS BIG OLD EASY chair in the library and cracked open the *The Bacchae* for the quiz the next day. My calculus tutor was at another table, figuring out the dimensions of the universe. A few other kids sat at a long wooden table, reading beneath bankers' lamps, but for the most part, the huge room was empty.

The random percussion of steam radiators provided a lulling soundtrack. You could put that in a song, I thought. I could hear the crackle of a fireplace somewhere. For once, I felt like I could have been anywhere except Oakhurst Hall: some really cool living room from a movie or something.

Once Simon had explained the play and I started to figure out how to read the words, I thought it was a pretty cool story. I was starting to get into ancient Greece. Any civilization that liked sports and wine couldn't be all bad—except that, like Bruno said, Greece ended in civil war and brought itself down . . .

I closed my eyes, and I was just sort of melting into the chair . . .

. . . while my brain was trying out a few more thoughts before I fell asleep . . . like . . .

. . . what Sam said . . . no matter where you go, there . . .

. . . and then I woke up with a start. I'd dozed off. I was cold, and the place was completely empty. I walked back to the dorm. Ward was waiting outside the door.

By now I'd figured out that The Hall had three kinds of faculty: the Jarvis ones trying to help you out by sharing what they'd learned in life, the teachers who were treading water until they summoned enough guts to find a life, and the cops who'd decided to earn their chops by giving out enough tickets that someday they could wear a head-of-school bow tie at a private day school in Tulsa.

I'd blown curfew by a good fifteen minutes. And the cop was waiting outside Screwville. When I told Ward I'd been in the library, it sounded completely lame, even though it was the truth. I guess that happens a lot. But I knew I couldn't have come up with a lie that worked, not with the way he was looking at me.

"The library is closed, Lefferts." Even though it was cold, beads of sweat on his half-bald head caught the light from a lamppost. He was totally getting off on this.

"But it wasn't," I said. "I was reading my history homework, and I fell asleep, and nobody else was there. So I left. Hey, I *ran* back here, sir." Okay, slight exaggeration.

"Every minute you waste bullshitting, son," said Ward, "is another minute you're late."

"I'm not lying," I said, "*sir.*"

Ward daggered me in the eye. "Lefferts, I was boarding in sixth grade. I know the game. You think you can beat the house. But you're messing with something bigger than you think. This place has been around for centuries, and it'll be here long after you're gone." He paused for a really stupid dramatic effect. Then he actually pointed a finger in my face and said, "You have no idea what you're dealing with, boy."

Damned if I was going to get punished for doing my god-damned homework. "Mr. Ward, I was just studying history," I said. "I was reading *The Bacchae*—and that's just what the play is about—somebody trying to bust up a society—"

"That's good, Jack," snapped Ward. He was about to explode. "I suggest you study it harder. Because history tells us that places like Oakhurst Hall are the places that keep the history of Western civilization going. Without us, everything falls apart. Now, get your butt into your room."

I slogged upstairs. Western civilization. What was that? The history of Wyoming? The history of honkies?

I threw my pack against the wall of the room. Josh was lying on his bed reading a magazine with Eddie van Halen on the cover.

"Explain, guitar man," I said. "I haven't been caught for

breaking lots of major rules. And then I get busted for studying."

He laughed. "Welcome to life through the looking glass." Then he went back to the magazine and added, as if it didn't matter, "Oh, and I passed your message on to Simon and Danny. Seems like we're all in for sobriety."

"Seriously?"

"But, man, I gotta warn you—I'm not real good at reality."

After English I wanted to tell Caroline the good news, but I could tell that she wasn't in the mood. Booth—her Ward— had been riding her too. "In time trials, she was all over me, even though I went from seventh to fifth," she said. "I'm not 'social' enough. She senses an 'attitude' problem. She's right: it's *her* attitude that's a problem. She's totally fake. I guess I have to start buying into the Beauty-Industrial Complex. I'm supposed to wear some bra that costs five times what it's supposed to? Who could possibly care what my bra looks like?"

"You'd be surprised," I said.

Damn!

But she just smiled that shy smile, and elbowed me, and blushed. And suddenly the guy who'd ever wasted a thought about Lucy and her legs vanished into thin air.

". . . just so hypocritical. I mean, girls are supposed to be, like, equal and strong now, right? No more glass ceiling! But then everyone still tells us what we have to look like, and we *believe* them. It's like girls are expected to be, I don't know, good at . . . *everything* now . . . which makes it hard to be . . . *anything*."

"I think you're a lot of things," I said. "And fake isn't one of them."

"Sorry. I'll chill out. And, hey, I made the symphony. Third flute."

"Yeah?" I said. "Cool! So what are they playing for the Thanksgiving concert?"

"Beethoven's Fifth. Boring and easy. But I guess they don't want to take any chances if it's really going to be on TV. Apparently it might be more than local cable access. Like maybe out of Boston. I guess Carlton's got some contacts. And were you ever right about Hopper. What a pompous ass. I was supposed to be eternally grateful when he told me I'd made the team."

As we walked up the music building steps, I suddenly felt Caroline's hand touch mine, just a brush. In books, moments like that are always described as some sort of zap of current, but for me, it was just a warm rush, all over.

I glanced down to see if she was trying to put her hand in mine. But she'd shoved it back into the pouch of her sweatshirt.

After we'd gone inside, I turned around and walked right back outside. I was feeling too good to let Hopper bring me back to earth. I went for a walk, and the next thing I knew, I was down on the thirds soccer field, where Alex and I were scheduled to fleece Yacht Boy the next day after real practice—followed, I hoped, by another calculus lesson from my private tutor.

Surrounded by woods, at the foot of the mountain, how could it be that, all the way down here, I could still smell Caroline Callahan's hair?

DURING PRACTICE THE NEXT DAY, I was supposed to block for Anthony on the second series, but there was no one to block: the play had stopped. Madden was sitting on the ground holding his right ankle and yelling. "Jesus, Clune! What the hell . . ."

The big guy was standing over his quarterback. "Hey, man, I'm sorry. My bad. You okay?" Turned out Clune had pulled out to block early because Mancini had jumped the whistle, and then Clune had stepped on Madden's foot. Then Mancini sacked the quarterback, which he wasn't to supposed to do in practice. But that was Mancini. That was our Oakhurst Hall D. In real life, they'd have to be leashed.

Madden threw an arm around Bannion, and they limped off toward the locker room.

"All right," said Ward. "Griffin—you're it." The backup quarterback was a senior named Charlie Griffin, who'd never played a down in his two years on the varsity as far as I knew, but was apparently a hell of a third baseman in baseball, which is how he got here. The baseball field was called Griffin Field, so maybe that had something to do with something, too. In practice, he had an accurate arm, and he could run out of the pocket. I figured that he was just going through all the right moves until he inherited his share of Griffindom.

But in the huddle on the next play, I was surprised to hear him say, "Lefferts: Fake and go. Long."

Maybe he wanted to seize his moment. Sounded good to me. I broke slowly at the snap, jogged toward Thorn, turned around toward Griffin like I was watching a running play . . . then took off downfield, faking our BMOC out of his jock and breaking totally into the clear. But the pass was behind me, and as I slowed down, out of the corner of my eye, I saw Zowitzki, coming at me full speed. He shouldn't have been anywhere near the play, unless he wanted to lay a cheap hit on my knees.

Okay, not this time. This time it was my turn. I slowed down, pretended to wait for the ball—then threw my right forearm into his face mask, and as I pulled it back, I might have let a few fingers reach in, with an innocent claw. As he grabbed at his mask to get my hand off it, I stuck a foot out, and he went flying.

The pass flew over my head as I turned to trot back to the huddle.

Ward was beet-red. "What the hell was that, Lefferts? You don't worry about the man—you worry about the ball!"

"You know what it was about—sir. I'll play football if they'll play football."

When I lined up for the next play, Thorn walked to the line and up into my face. "Watch your ass, loser."

"I don't have to," I said. "It doesn't need needles." I expected him to fight. But he didn't. He didn't even try to cheap-shot me the rest of the practice, maybe because Ward had left to go check up on Madden, and now it was just Bruno watching practice.

"All right, listen up." Ward was standing next to the school emblem in the carpet in the locker room, because you weren't allowed to stand *on* it. "I know what you're thinking: St. Keelen's is a slam dunk, that we've got a W before we even play. Thinking ahead to Williamton. But Keelen's got some stuff this year. They've won their first two."

The God Squad was a school just a few counties away, known for turning out ministers and geniuses, but no one could remember when their football team had been serious.

"Against who?" twanged Addison. "Our Mother of the Bleeding Pussy?"

Bruno's voice sliced through the laughs. "You and I are going to talk. Now." The running back slunk over to the head coach's office, and Bruno slammed the door.

"So here's the deal," Ward said. "Madden's ankle's sprained. Nothing serious, but we can't risk it getting worse, so Griffin's gonna start. Which means we're gonna go heavy on the run. Like *nothing* but the run. Which means we're gonna be slamming right into a couple of very religious PGs they signed this year from New Jersey. These guys are huge. Don't take these mothers lightly."

The St. Keelen's campus was like something out of an English movie about the Knights of the Round Table: towers, arches, a giant cathedral with a golden spire.

"Jesus," Anthony said, as we drove across a stone bridge over a bubbling stream. "Looks like monks live here. Really rich monks."

Bruno and Ward had gathered us under this huge maple tree with perfect autumn yellow-orange leaves. It didn't seem like a place for a pep talk. All Bruno said was, "That's a hell of a tree, isn't it?" as he looked up through the branches. "Gotta be a couple hundred years old."

I saw Thorn and Zowitzki look at each other like the guy was insane. I was still trying to figure the man out. Maybe Ward was the hand puppet, and Bruno the ventriloquist.

Even Ward's talk didn't have much pep. He was either superconfident or Bruno had told him to keep it calm. Ward just said, "Let's stomp 'em!"

In the first quarter, the St. Keelen's offense *was* playing like a bunch of monks. Mancini sacked their quarterback three times in the first five minutes. But, like Ward had said, the St. Keelen's defensive line averaged about three hundred pounds, and their outside linebackers were quick. At first, our offense was spinning its wheels. Addison and Anthony were running into brick walls.

I got into the game midway through the second quarter. Griffin didn't call my number on the first few series. But I noticed that the St. Keelen's cornerback's first step was to the inside. He was always watching my feet to see what I'd do. I told Griffin, and he called for a bomb.

This was it. His pass was a perfect, arching spiral, falling out of the sky. It kissed my palms . . . just as the safety slammed me from the blindside. The ball popped out. Incomplete.

"Nice hands, Lefferts," Addison growled as we walked to the sideline. I ignored him. I was too pissed at myself to say anything.

But when we got the ball back, I was in again. This time, Griffin hit me on a square out: my first official catch!—and good for a first down. As I ran out of bounds, through the St. Keelen's team, I *so* wanted to spike the ball at their feet. But I didn't. As someone once said, "Act like you've been there before."

And now I'd been there. I had a catch.

It was Will's turn next: Griffin hit him in stride across the middle, and the big kid juked his way to the five. Addison scored on a burst up the middle.

On the next series, Thorn forced a fumble on a screen

pass, Zowitzki scooped it up and took it in, and we led 14–0 at the half.

We huddled back under the tree. I wondered what Ward was going to decide to poke a hole in. It didn't take long to find out. "Football is winning the war on the ground. And our ground game has to start picking it up. I want to see some pancake blocks out there." But everyone figured that we had the game won. The St. Keelen's offense didn't have a single first down.

This time, Zowitzki didn't say anything. But he did wander over to Griffin. At first, Griffin shook his head. Then he shrugged his shoulders and nodded. Something was up.

In the third quarter, St. Keelen's carved out a touchdown when one of their three-hundred-pounders broke through and hit Griffin just as he was handing the ball to Addison. The ball popped into the air, and the kid gathered it in and rambled forty yards, outrunning our entire offense in pursuit, including Will and Bannion, who pulled up hobbling as he chased the huge kid.

So it was 14–7 entering the fourth quarter. With Bannion out, I played every down. And Griffin never looked my way again. Play after play, I fumed in the huddle while Griffin called everyone's name but my own. Zowitzki must have told Griffin not to throw it to me.

Then, with five minutes to go, St. Keelen's defense stopped us in our own end, blocked the punt, and their other giant lineman fell on it, got up, and rambled twenty yards into the end zone. I turned around and took off after him, but it was way too late. Will and I reached the end zone together, after the kid had already scored.

Ward was the color of a tomato. This could be a long bus ride home. If we even *tied* the God Squad . . . and I realized as we took the field, I cared. I wasn't following, or wandering, or idling. I was a part of this team. And so when Griffin called for a screen pass to Addison, going to my side, I leveled the cornerback with a crazy block, hopped up, ran downfield, and threw a second block on the safety.

Addison took it all the way for the winning touchdown.

Back on the sideline, Griffin was the first to high-five me. Then Will, Anthony, and Clune. Madden, in street clothes, gave me a nod as I walked to the Gatorade bucket. I nodded back.

In the final minute, Mancini sacked the St. Keelen's quarterback on third down, and, on the last play, Zowitzki leveled him on a blitz. Aiming for the poor kid's head with his own. I think the kid is still lying there.

We'd squeaked it out.

Before the postgame talk, I saw Bruno talking to Ward, and after that, Ward was weirdly calm. We should have beaten them by thirty. We'd let him down. And I should have caught that bomb. I guess I'd started to believe my hands really *were* magic.

Bruno opened by praising Griffin for stepping in and holding the fort. And all Ward said was, "You dodged a bullet today. You weren't ready. Maybe it's a lesson you needed. Still, you won. So we'll take it. But put it away. Williamton's gonna be a buzz saw." Williamton was a huge school from northern Connecticut, a third-rate factory for academics, but with a huge enrollment, which meant they had depth.

"They're undefeated. Their defense is giving up six points a game. And unless you spend every minute of the next week with your head in that game, you're going to make fools of yourselves in front of your families and the alums."

"Nice positive feedback," I said to Anthony, as we climbed onto the bus.

"Stay cool. You laid some killer blocks. And you got your first stat, man: Lefferts, one reception, five yards."

I was in the history books—yeah, maybe to be buried in some basement shelf full of old record books where my stat would gather dust, but today, I'd take it. And I still kinda wished I'd spiked it at the God Squad's sideline.

It was just getting dark when the bus pulled in. Our band was going to practice, but first I called home to tell Dad about how things had started to go okay. He wanted to tell me about how he'd landed the Kansas City stadium gig. It was always about him. I guess it meant a whole lot of bucks. "But it also means I'm going to be spending a lot of time out in the boonies," he said.

"We've only got three games left," I said. "I mean, if you wanted to catch one."

I guessed that the silence meant he wasn't totally into the idea of driving seven hours to see me sit on the bench. "There's always next year," he said.

I hadn't thought about next year much. "Well, what about the last day of the term before Thanksgiving break?" I said. "We play Essex, maybe for the championship, then there's this huge concert. You'll be here for that, right?"

He said he had to check his calendar. And that he could always send a limo to bring me home. I'd like to have a chauffeur, right?

Right. Sure.

I told him to say hi to Grace.

"She said to tell you not to break any bones. And I don't want you breaking too many hearts." He laughed.

I told him I'd try not to. I also didn't tell him I hoped it wasn't going to be the other way around.

THEY WERE ALL WAITING FOR ME. And I could tell that my edict hadn't made Danny real happy. "So we're doing this straight now?" he said. "Because you say so?"

Josh waited for me to speak.

"Look," I said, "it's not like I'm telling you what to do on your time. Just *ours*."

"Gee," Danny said, "that's big of you. You're just a part-time sponsor, huh?"

"Look," I said. "I don't know what else you've got going on, but I'm tanking French, I don't have a girl, and I got a fucking Nazi who reams me every day while my own teammates are trying to kill me and then stays on my ass in the dorm." No reply. "So I'm gonna ride the music as far as I can. But it'd be cool if we could all ride it to the top. We're good enough. You know we are."

Danny loosened up with a smile. "I feel your pain. I'm pulling a D in chem, I got *two* demerits for turning in a fake phone. And my girl back home just dropped me by Twitter."

Simon was rocking back and forth with his hands in his

pockets, waiting to see where this was going to go, enjoying every second of it: these silly humans.

"Look," I said, "you seem to be pretty good on that bass, and I'm guessing you didn't get there snorting Ritalin while you learned it. Or smoking weed every time you picked up your axe. It's like juicing in football. It's fake, it's a crutch."

Finally, Josh joined in. "I mean, everybody's got a band. But how many of them ever make it out of the garage?"

"Vanilla icing from the can tastes great if you're stoned," Simon said, nodding, to back me up, "but you don't see it on restaurant menus. You write a riff on weed, or Stoli, or coke? Of *course* it's going to sound good. But not to a label."

"A label? Dude," said Danny, "we don't even have a name."

Everyone was quiet.

"The Others," said Josh. "That's what we are. We're not the class officers, or the captains, or the scholars. We're Oakhurst Hall's Others. We'll probably be the other kids in college too. So let's own it."

I liked it. Danny and Simon slapped hands. Josh flashed me a peace sign. All was cool again.

And this time our new song, or mini symphony, or soundtrack, or whatever the hell it was, began to sound as if it had been written by someone with at least a clue. It had two movements. It needed a third. Other than that, I thought, as I listened to Josh noodle a less-frantic-than-usual lead, it was coolly unclassifiable.

We stopped to rework a few sections and changed a few chords, and, for the first time, it felt like we were actually rehearsing. Finally, we were doing the work.

When we left the building, Josh and Simon split off. I think they wanted me and Danny to smooth things over. We walked back toward the quad.

"Hey," he said, "I didn't mean to put you down. I don't take well to authority, you know? Never played nice with the other kids in the sandbox."

We bumped fists. "So how'd *you* end up here?"

"I wish I knew," he said. "My dad's business was going down, and we had to move to this really grotty part of Philly. He wanted me out of there. Somehow he got me in on a full ride because I was a science freak. I loved chem. Like a puzzle that, if you solved it, you could get to the next level and then cure cancer or something. Turns out I get here and all the teachers care about is hammering the curriculum into you so that when you get to the next level, you don't fuck up and make them look bad. So mostly I sat in my room with the lights off and the amp on."

Playing the cards they deal you. We walked in silence for a few minutes. Then I asked, "So you're going to stick it out?"

"It's this or somewhere in South Philly where I get my geek ass kicked every day. The band makes it easier. Maybe you're the kick in the ass we all needed."

• • •

The next night after dinner I decided to wander over to Caroline's dorm: Thompson-Aaron. Or T&A, to the football team. I felt like celebrating: the band had turned a corner, even if I didn't know what we were heading for, and I wanted to tell her about my catch on Saturday. In front of her dorm, I sat down with my back to a big maple, crunching the leaves. Maybe I'd luck out and catch her coming in.

Or maybe I'd just meditate. How *did* you meditate, anyway? Simon did it. He told me the whole point was to stop thinking. So I tried to picture blankness. At first all I could see was Caroline's little half smile. But after a few minutes, I actually heard the sound of leaves falling, one by one, every few seconds, scraping through the other leaves in the trees. It was sort of musical.

Then I heard footsteps and looked up to see a girl wearing a funky bright blue jacket with a bowling team name stitched on the front, a hippie skirt, and earphones.

"Hi, I'm Jack," I said.

"I'm Chloe," she said, pulling out the phones. I heard the echoes of Regina Spektor. Chloe was short and had a pretty, pixieish round face and cool-dorky glasses. I asked her if she knew Caroline.

"Yeah. She's, like, the coolest. Why?"

"What's her room number?"

She looked at me like I was out of my mind. "Four

fourteen. But it's Booth's floor, you know. And you're not supposed to—"

"Yeah," I said. "I know."

She shrugged and stuck the earphones back in her ears. "Good luck," she said.

I was feeling too good not to try it. Time to seize the day.

I bounced up the carpeted stairs two at a time, reached the fourth floor, opened the door, and peeked down the corridor: Booth's door was closed.

Room 414 had a poster on it of that painting with three people in a diner in the middle of the night. I knocked. She was wearing a sweatshirt and sweatpants, her hair pulled into a ponytail. "What are you *doing* here?" she said. "This is stupid, Jack. Booth's a bitch. If she catches you . . ." She pulled me in by my sweatshirt and closed the door. "So whatever you have to say couldn't have waited?"

What *did* I have to say? Wait, that was easy. "I just wanted to know if . . . if we, you know, are . . . I don't know . . ."

"You're going to have to learn how to finish a sentence, Lefferts, if Jarvis is going to give you an A."

We stood there, stupidly. Then she reached out both her hands, with her palms up. So I put my hands in hers. And maybe *then* there was some sort of current. It was definitely electric. For me, anyway. She was just totally cool and relaxed.

"We're *something*," she said. "Why do you have to label

it? Now, get out of here. All we need is Booth busting me. Or you."

I bounced down the stairs. It was good. Another corner turned—and this one might lead to a really cool horizon. If I didn't mess it up. If I just kept being the me that was starting to wake up.

Back in Screwville, I grabbed the Gershwin prelude sheet music, walked over to the arts building, sat down at Hopper's piano and worked on the allegro with its five goddamned sharps. And now, instead of the music challenging me, I was challenging the music. These three little songs were the first music I'd ever played where I could actually feel the emotion while I was playing the stuff. I'd played a million old songs without having a clue what the guys in the wigs had been thinking when they wrote them, but now I was channeling some dude from less than a century ago. An American dude. I nailed the allegro. *Nailed* it. Then I sat still, listening to the after tones in the room. Like adrenaline sweetly calming down after a good football play.

The more I thought about auditioning for the concert, the more I knew I didn't want to. This was music I kind of wanted to keep for myself. For nights like this. Except maybe with someone else listening. This flute player I knew.

I didn't want to leave yet. I didn't want this high to end. I started playing the band's song, with the Schubert and the birdsong . . . and then the hard-rock song we'd come up with on Jack Daniel's night . . .

And then, out of the blue, I bopped some keys, randomly, with my right hand, bouncing around, throwing in a sharp here and there where you wouldn't expect it—and I found the beginnings of a new melody, in the same key as the other things we'd written, for the final movement.

I don't know where it came from, except maybe room 414 in T&A. I do know that it sounded like it was written by someone who had finished the journey as a different person than when he'd started it.

It was simple, the melody, and it was sort of sad and happy at the same time. I closed my eyes and played it again and again and again, letting my hands do the thinking as my brain went over the images of the last few days: the killer blocks that sprang the winning touchdown against St. Keelen's. Me getting in Ward's face. In Hopper's face.

Me knowing that things like Ward and weed were stupid back roads, as in looking back. That somewhere down the road, there was a calm.

I was smiling when I finished it. And if sounded a little corny, well, sue me.

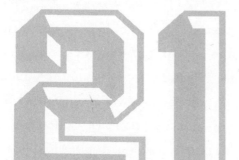

BY NOW I BARELY NOTICED THE weight room's gym chemical sweat and a soundtrack like *Poison's Greatest Hits*. But it was hard to ignore Zowitzki, who was now in my face with an ultimatum after practice.

"Listen, Lefferts," he said, "if it makes you feel any better, you'd be in very good company. A couple of guys who might surprise you."

"I've never been real good at going with the crowd," I said.

He shook his head. "Man, you are making *such* a mistake." And he walked away.

That sort of ruined my session. I benched the weight and walked out the door . . . and kept walking. Down the long, winding entrance and right out to the real world.

Somebody'd told me that Jarvis lived just off campus. So I took a right, on Concord County Highway 63A, which headed a few miles down to what passed for the village of Engleside, which was basically a general store, a pizza place, a gas station, and a couple of nice churches. I wasn't actually allowed to walk off campus. Only A-students had "town privileges." But if Ward wanted to drive past me and bust me then . . . fine.

I tried to listen to the peepers somewhere in the ditch in front of the cornfield so I could stop imagining stomping Zowitzki's head into mush. Then I saw JARVIS stenciled onto a black metal mailbox in front of a muddy driveway that led to a big, rambling old house. Wicker chairs with faded paint filled the porch, facing in every direction, just like his classroom.

Jarvis answered the buzzy old doorbell wearing a plain white T-shirt and smoking an unfiltered cigarette.

"Jack. What's up? Come on in," Jarvis said, turning around and walking down a hallway next to some old wooden stairs, like it was totally normal that some kid would show up on his doorstep.

I followed him into this room with papers sliding off desks and tables, books sliding out bookshelves, a shelf of vinyl records, coffee cups with rings of evaporated coffee, CDs in random piles. An old poster tacked to the wall said LET GO, OR BE DRAGGED and the name of some Buddhist temple.

He swept a few books off an old leather wingback chair that a cat had clawed into shreds. Then he slumped into the chair behind his desk and slipped a Benny Goodman CD into a boom box as old as the one in the classroom. The bookshelf had a whole section of sci-fi novels by V. R. Hamilton. I recognized the name from the fantasy section at the Barnes & Noble on the Upper East Side. Luke loved that writer. He'd read every book the guy had ever written, which was, like, a dozen. This felt like home.

"So what's up?" he said. "You need an extension on the short story? Take another week."

"Thanks." I said. I didn't say anything else. I wasn't sure what I wanted to say. But when he spoke again, it was like he'd read my mind.

"Things okay at home?" He stabbed his cigarette butt into an ashtray that said "I Got a Rush from Mount Rushmore."

"Yeah," I said. "I guess. How come you have all this stuff from all these states?"

"Read Kerouac a lot. Now road trips are my religion." He lit another cigarette and waited for me to say something. So I told him about my dad. Not that there was much to tell. I mean, it didn't sound like too many kids around here had real relationships with their parents anyway. But still. It was weird that Dad hadn't even e-mailed me. Then, I hadn't e-mailed him either.

"My guess is your dad is still too new at parenthood to know that he's trying to live his life through you," Jarvis said. "I did that with my first kid. Fortunately, it didn't work. Stick it out. He'll grow up and see what he was doing, and hope-fully, when he's finally happy with himself, he'll be happy with you."

Jarvis's wife walked into the room. She had a happy, lined face and brown hair with gray streaks in it. She was wearing blue-jean overalls covered in dirt. Jarvis introduced us.

"Jack! Johnny has talked about you."

Johnny? Johnny Jarvis. Sounded like a pro tennis player,

instead of a fringe prep teacher. I stood up and shook her hand. "Glad to meet you."

"Nice of you to drop by on such a glorious day. Honey, I'm going to get a little garden time in before it gets dark, if you need me," she said. "Otherwise we'll have no garlic at all next July!" And she was gone.

"So you guys are doing *The Bacchae* in history? Great stuff." He puffed out circles of smoke, which drifted apart in the late-afternoon sun coming through the window. "Kingdoms don't work out so well in the long run. But you can't have people running around just having fun all the time, either, can you? Like this place. For starters."

"You mean Oakhurst Hall is the kingdom?"

"Well, yeah," he said. "But imagine if I ran this place. It'd be anarchy, right? Crazy old English teacher."

"I don't think so," I said.

"Oh, yeah," he said. Then he stood up, like he had something more important do to, so I did too. "My advice?" he said. "Keep your eyes and ears open. Listen when you hear something that makes sense, and ignore the rest."

We walked down his hallway. "One other thing, Jack," he said, as we reached the old heavy wood front door of his house. This sounded like it was going to be heavy. "I don't know why you don't have the confidence to lead discussions or offer opinions. I wasn't there for the first fifteen years of your life. But . . . this place needs kids like you. Take off the muzzle."

"I'm trying," I said. It sounded true. He opened that heavy, creaky door.

"Sir? Can I ask you a question? When you talked about me to your wife . . . what did you say?"

Jarvis paused, as if he had to remember. "I guess I told her about that your take on the Gatsby paper was the one I've been waiting twenty years for and couldn't figure out myself. That it's simple: The reason rich people end up so unhappy is because they've never had the balls to aim higher than the safety of the dollars." Then he shrugged, as if that was obvious.

"Thanks," I said. "And V. R. Hamilton? All those books? Is he good?"

"Some of the reviewers thought so. But the pay sucks."

V. R. Hamilton was Johnny Jarvis! "My best friend really likes your books, sir."

He smiled. "Tell him I'm almost done with *The Lyco-cambrian Mythos, Part VII: Creep in Wolf's Clothing.*" Then he laughed. "I leave the real literature to the people with vision. The ones who are smart enough to create things that change the world."

Maybe I was imagining it. Or maybe he looked me straight in the eye before he closed the big, old wooden door.

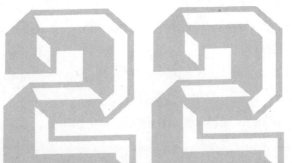

THE NEXT DAY I PLAYED A Chopin étude from memory for Hopper—simple, but with some sort of feeling that I owned the notes, instead of them owning me.

"Where has *that* been?" Hopper was smiling. It didn't seem to suit his face. "That was the first time you've played with any passion since you entered this room. This is *you* speaking."

"Articulating?" I said, smiling.

"Exactly!" Hopper said. "Now, Jack, are you still thinking of actually playing the Gershwin for the final audition? It's going to be very hard for me to judge you against Mario Miles if you're playing some eight-minute piece that George seems to have written in his spare time."

Apparently they were on a first-name basis. Even if George had died in 1937.

"You could master a Brahms concerto in a week if you put your mind to it. You know that. Mario knows that too."

It was all about Mario for Hopper. I knew that now. And from the look on his face, I think he knew he'd overplayed his hand. He didn't want me to win as much as he wanted Mario to lose.

"Mr. Hopper," I said, "the piano's never been about competing for me. Shouldn't it just be enough that I like playing?"

He knew I had him.

"Well, yes, of course. To a point. But after that point, if you're serious about your craft, you'll be rudely awakened to the fact that it's a cutthroat world, Jack. And our job is to get you ready for that world."

"But what if I don't want to enter the Van Cliburn Competition?" I said. "What if I don't want to become a symphony pianist?"

For the first time since I'd known him, Hopper looked almost sad, or . . . beaten. Not just because my success could have been a reflection on his success. But because, maybe on some level, he knew that living through someone else meant you hadn't lived for yourself.

"Jack, you have real talent and a very good ear. All the greats do. You need schooling, but you have tools. It's a shame you haven't been studying with some real masters until now. But we can make up for the lost time. Why wouldn't you want to push yourself, knowing the rewards of being elite?"

"Because it takes the fun out of it," I said.

He let out a long breath. I think he was weighing his options. So he went into default mode. "If I were you," he said, "I'd start thinking about all the people you'd be letting down. That evening before the Thanksiving break is not just another recital, young man. It's a night of pride in

the school. For many, it's the most important night of the entire school year. Every one of those musicians deserves to be
playing with our very best. It's not about you, Jack. It's about
Oakhurst Hall."

Well, I'd heard that enough by now. "I don't think I'm
cut out to be one of those guys who goes out front and flips
the tails of his tux before he sits down," I said.

"Then you're wasting my time, aren't you?" Hopper said,
in a frozen-cold voice. He turned to gaze out the window.

"I guess I am," I said. This time it was my turn to push
away from the piano and leave the room.

I hit the practice room a half hour before band practice that
night, and the door opened a minute later. It was Mario,
with his pack, wearing a red sweatshirt with the hammer
and sickle of the Russian flag on it

"Hey, mind if I listen?" Mario said. "What are you playing? It was really sweet." This wasn't the Mario with attitude.
The kid seemed lonely. I was glad to have someone to talk
to. Especially the kid Hopper seemed determined to keep
down.

"Gershwin. Real nice stuff. What, you *live* over here?" I
said, smiling.

"Yeah," Mario said, smiling self-consciously, flashing a
row of braces with different colored rubber bands. "Home
away from home. I don't have a lot of friends. My mom says

that I'll make friends in college, where there'll be other kids like me, but I don't think there really *are* other kids like me. Even at Juilliard, or Berklee. I think people like me belong somewhere else."

I'd had the same thought. I wanted to say so, but I let him go on. He seemed to need to tell his tale to someone. And I wanted to hear it.

"You know what I think about doing sometimes for next year? Just taking off, hitchhiking around Europe. Playing the piano in bars and dives and restaurants. Learning jazz. Having fun."

It didn't sound crazy to me at all. It sounded like heaven.

"Hey, do you mind if I . . ." Mario was eyeing the sheet music. "I've never played any Gershwin."

"Seriously? Be my guest," I said.

Mario sat at the bench, and studied each of the four pages of sheet music for about fifteen seconds each. Then he just played the whole allegro, with maybe three or four mistakes, max. First time out.

"Jesus," was all I could say. "That was amazing."

"Naw," said Mario, blushing. "It'd be amazing if I *hadn't* been able to do that. There's no separation between my brain and my hands. The music is just software. My hands do what my brain tells them. There's no thought involved. Apparently, I have something of the idiot savant to me. Sometimes I think it's more just the idiot part."

He slung his pack and headed for the door. "Hey, stick around," I said. "How'd you end up here? I'm doing a survey."

He sat in a chair, but he kept his pack in his lap. "My dad was one of the guys who created MySpace, so they took me even though I had a C-minus average and about ten years of being in therapy. What they didn't know is that he blew the whole thing on gambling and coke and sort of disappeared. He's somewhere in the Caribbean. By the second year, we couldn't pay the tuition, but they figured my expertise at the old piano might give them some payback and they gave me a ride."

"And so?"

"And so what happened to my dad sort of made me see things differently. I mean, what money does. They were always saying I should do something extracurricular, so I founded the Secondary School Socialists' Club and tried to organize other schools in New England. We had about 100 members before they shut it down."

He got up. He wasn't real comfortable with other people, I guess. "What about you?"

"Me? Minor-league version of your story. My dad stuck around. Then he wanted a prep school on his resume. Hey, how come you never studied with Hopper?"

"I did," he said, opening the door to leave. "After one lesson, he refused to teach me anymore. Said I was 'insolent.' Funny. That's probably the only thing I'm not."

• • •

A few minutes later, the rest of the band filed into the room. None of them seemed completely into it. Maybe I'd turned this into just another class? Maybe everyone deserved a day off.

So while they plugged in their instruments, I started playing the blues on the bass clef. Just the down-and-out, dirty blues: E-A-B. Maybe it was Jimmy Rodgers's "Walking by Myself," or maybe it was Johnny Winter playing Robert Johnson. Didn't matter. It was just the blues—the kind of stuff that people probably played in bad bars for hours in Kansas City, jamming and ordering pitchers and feeling good.

It was Simon who got it first, backing me on drums. Danny started fingering simple bass notes. And Josh, nodding crazily, started playing blues leads he'd probably learned from some South Side Chicago guy at a club he'd gotten into with a fake ID. All I knew was that it sounded great.

Then, about five minutes into it, the drums stopped. Simon was tapping his sticks together like someone tapping their glass to make a toast. We all stopped and looked at the goofiest member of our quartet.

And then, when he had our attention, he slid into the opening of our little symphony. Playtime was over.

Danny's bass followed, I came in with the Schubert, and Josh started strumming the chords. I tried not to smile. This was very cool. It wasn't some Hopper saying, "All right, enough fooling around, turn to the pianissimo forte." It was four kids, alone, but maybe getting to be bigger than the sum of their parts. A team.

We played. The first version went pretty well, and I added in the third movement, the one I'd written after visiting T&A. The rest of the guys picked it up, Josh echoing me on guitar. Then we started from the beginning again. The second time through, I noticed that Danny had closed his eyes, and was nodding to himself with the really good sections, then, at the end, opened his eyes and looked at each of us separately, nodding encouragement, And we brought that puppy home.

Then we packed up in silence. I swear—I don't think we'd spoken a single word.

On the walk back to the campus, Danny stopped, pulled a joint from the pocket of his pink oxford Brooks Brothers shirt, lit it, and passed it to me: a peace offering, in a way. I took a small hit and passed it on to Josh, and the four of us walked back to Oakhurst Hall's version of civilization, each in our own space, but together—like that Revolutionary War painting with the two drummers and the guy in a bandage playing some kind of flute, and someone with a flag behind them. Too bad no one took a picture. I had a feeling we'd want to look back on this night someday.

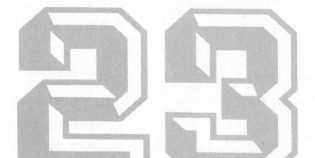

THE DAY OF THE WILLIAMTON GAME dawned cool and windy. There was a good cold feel to the air, and the hillside was filling up while we went through warm-ups: the Abercrombies cracking out their state-of-the-art folding chairs with the little cup-holder things stitched into the armrests.

But this time it was the mountain that caught my eye, with its quilt of orange and yellow and red leaves. All week the trees had been turning, like someone was colorizing a black-and-white movie. Like Kansas becoming the yellow brick road. Like everything coming into a little more focus.

I spied the Lucy posse and Carlton's group, then, up at the top of the hill, Caroline, with the Chloe girl at her side. Which automatically made it a great day for a football game.

But I still spent most of the first half on the sideline, watching us struggle against the school from Connecticut. These guys were so huge it was ridiculous. The rumor was that earlier in the year, when they'd shown up for a game down at some small school in Rhode Island, the head took one look at Williamton and called the game off because he didn't want his kids to get killed.

They showed up at our place with all-black uniforms, a half dozen ranting, red-faced coaches, and a crowd of lunatic alums. And from the beginning, they played like a team possessed. Their offensive line was not only big, they were disciplined and they knew their techniques. Their center stood up to Maniac Mancini, which no one had done yet, and their running backs ground out steady yardage. Their defense were headhunters.

After his week off, Madden was skittish in the pocket, overthrowing Will three times in the first three series. Even Addison was getting stuffed at the line.

I got in for two series, but Madden never looked my way. On his best throw, deep in Williamton's end, when he finally figured he had to throw to Bannion, he found him wide open down the middle. Bannion dropped it. Since he was also our kicker and had clearly decided to just survive the day without anyone actually hitting him, hurting him, or even running into him, he also missed a chip-shot field goal.

At the half, we were down 14–0, the first time we'd been behind in a game all season. As we gathered beneath the goalposts at the base of the mountain, for the first time that year, I felt the cockiness leaking out of the team.

Bruno's speech, as usual, was short, and to the point: "You're going to have to dig a little deeper inside yourselves today, aren't you?" Then he walked away and Ward took over.

This time, the drill sergeant didn't even open his mouth.

He just looked at us like we were lepers, turned back toward the field, and sailed his clipboard like a Frisbee. It went a surprisingly long distance. When he turned around, he was scary calm.

"That's what you're doing: throwing away everything we've worked for. The perfect season. The championship. Your college scholarships. Hey, it's your lives, not mine. I got time. I got tenure. Couple years from now, maybe I'll get a gang that wants to win."

Just then—you couldn't have timed it better with a movie script—a loud guitar chord cut through the air, from somewhere up the mountain. Then another chord. Then a couple of drum strokes . . . and suddenly I was listening to the hard-rock middle section of our song. Josh and Danny and Simon must have dragged some battery-powered amps and a drum set up into the hills. Unreal. Who'd have thought the mountains had such good acoustics?

"What the hell is *that*?" Ward shouted. I turned around so Ward couldn't see the grin beneath my face mask. The coach turned his back in disgust and started to walk back to the sideline. Most of the team followed him, led by Zowitzki.

But a half dozen of them stayed behind, to listen—including Madden.

Right on cue, the song moved into the final section, with Josh's guitar playing part of the quiet ending that would have been my piano.

And then a few pockets of parents started breaking into applause, and some of the kids shouted out some props. They'd *liked* it!

When the last note died away from the mountain, Madden walked over to me, his long blond hair matted to his forehead. "You got some balls, Lefferts."

"Glad you liked it."

"I didn't say I liked it," said the quarterback. "I said you had balls."

I wasn't about to tell him I'd had no idea what was going to happen.

"You wouldn't know anything about that, would you?" Will asked as we put on our helmets.

"Not a thing," I said, with a cat-swallowing-the-canary look. If they all wanted to think I'd done it, that was way okay with me.

"I always thought we should have a marching band, anyway," Will said. "I guess this'll do."

On the sideline, Ward turned to me. "Lefferts, you're starting the second half. Bannion's hurting." Maybe his self-esteem had been bruised. Or his dad was threatening to cut off the inheritance. I didn't care. All I knew was that Caroline and her friend were up there somewhere on the hill, and I was so amped on the sideline, looking to the faces in the hillside as we took the kickoff, that it took me a second to notice that Anthony had gathered in the short kickoff, and was now bowling right up the middle—and running all the way to the end zone.

Garver! The Prep for Prepster! A seventy-yard kick-return for a TD!

Then, on Williamton's first series, after a couple of first downs, Mancini finally broke through their line, picked up their running back, and squeezed him so hard the ball popped loose, like a grape. Zowitzki fell on it, and we had it right back at midfield.

It was a ball game. Down just one touchdown. I was psyched for all the right reasons: we might *win* this thing.

On our next offensive series, Madden called the reverse. "For real?" I said.

"Just run the play," he said. That sounded real.

At the snap, I broke back toward the quarterback, and this time, Madden actually handed me the ball. I looked up-field. I saw a tall linebacker, and his mistake was trying to take my head off with a clothesline. I ducked beneath his swipe.

Now a cornerback lowered his head, but he'd mistimed my speed, and I shook off his half tackle as I broke for the sideline. I'd gained twenty yards before the safety came over, took the perfect angle, and tackled me hard, lowering his shoulders at my knees. I flipped into the air and landed hard on my back. But I still had the ball.

As I trotted back to the huddle, I heard a few cheers and

let them wash over me. Then, Caroline's voice, above it all: "Yeah, number eighty-eight!"

Clune's high five sealed the deal in the huddle.

From then on, we were a completely different team. The second-rate monsters were wilting. The louder their coaches screamed at them, the more they seemed to lose their manic high. Maybe the coke was wearing off. Addison and Anthony started finding holes. Madden found me on a curl-in for one first down: my second catch! Then he hit Will for the tying touchdown on a fade pattern from the fifteen. Tied at 14–14.

The next twenty minutes were a war game, with no one giving up any yardage in the trenches. With four minutes left, Addison came up six inches short on a fourth-and-one on their thirty, and we turned it over.

"Our turn! Our turn!" said Zowitzki, head-bumping the defense on the sideline. On Williamton's next possession, their quarterback went for it all. Their end had Thorn beat, but the guy underthrew the ball, Thorn caught up, reached up, and picked it off: a highlight play.

In the next huddle, Madden wanted it all back and called a deep cross to Will—but then we heard the whistle. Bruno or Ward had called a time-out. Anthony sprinted in: "Bruno says all runs. All the time."

Madden looked at him, and I could tell he was wondering whether to ignore the command. He did the right thing. First he called a running play for Anthony, who followed Clune's block and juked for six yards. And for the next eight plays, Anthony and Addison substituted for each other on each play, and somehow, some way, each run gained more. The Williamton guys were exhausted. The hillside was now a rolling thunder of cheers.

We got it down to the ten. Now we were facing first and goal. But a field goal wasn't an option—Bannion was hurt. We needed some way to get the ball into the end zone in four plays.

On first down, Addison hit the line, and I swear, he was screaming, and—call it 'roid rage, or maybe just guts—he refused to go down. He lowered his head, the whole pack began to move, like rugby, with all of us kind of pushing, and then next thing you knew, he was in: touchdown.

Game!

I was getting slapped on the pads, on the helmet, swirling in the maelstrom. We all moved down to the end zone for Ward's sermon.

"Don't get overconfident on me now," he growled. "We've got a week off. If you don't spend every hour of the next two weeks thinking about Anglican, then the Essex game on the last day won't be for the frickin' championship. So I'm giving you the heads-up. Tuesday's practice is going to be intense."

I was looking for Caroline and Chloe as the crowd thinned out, but there was no sign of them. It was hard to miss Lucy, though, as she and her friends surrounded Madden.

"Jack!" It was McGregor, the admissions guy. I hadn't

spoken to him since the day I'd had that interview, six months before. "Nice game, Jack! Great to see you out there," he said, offering a pink-skinned handshake. "It's always encouraging to see our students take advantage of everything we have to offer here. There's nothing like being on a team, bonding in a locker room."

His grin looked like he was posing for a portrait or something. "And how's that piano going? We going to hear you at the Thanksgiving concert?"

"Well, I don't know, sir," I said. "But I'm in this band, and we're writing a really nice song."

"That wouldn't have anything to do with our halftime serenade, would it?"

"Um . . . maybe," I said.

And I suddenly I had this thought. And it was insane.

"Really," McGregor said. "I've never heard anything quite like it." Then he loped off to talk to some parents on the hillside.

I walked up the hill with Anthony.

"Looks like your band gave us a boot in the butt," he said.

"No," I said, "your kickoff return gave us the boot."

"If that's not on *SportsCenter*'s Top Ten Plays tonight, I'm gonna sue."

Josh, Danny, and Simon were waiting outside the locker room. "How'd it sound from down here?" Josh asked.

"Sweet," I said. "But you could have used a keyboard. So how come didn't you tell me you were going to play?"

"Because you'd have told us not to," Josh said. He was right. "But don't feel like we left you out. You can help us carry the equipment back down."

Caroline and Chloe were waiting after I'd showered. I was hoping for a hug or a shoulder-bump, but Caroline just gave me a high five.

"That was so cool!" Chloe said. "Your band is awesome!"

"Let's hope Carlton appreciated it," I said. "And doesn't come down heavy."

"What's he going to bust them for?" Caroline said. "Illegal music?"

"He'll find a way," I said, because I knew he would.

And he did, in the next morning's sermon: "'A dim old wood, with a palace rare hidden away in its depths somewhere!' The poet, of course, is James Whitcomb Riley—and even though he wasn't writing about Oakhurst Hall, he might as well have been. We do live in a palace, overlooked by these glorious woods. And those woods are a special part of our campus."

"Uh-oh," said Sam, giving me an elbow. "This is about your boys."

"Now, I don't want you to think I'm opposed to the

occasional prank," Carlton said. "But I would encourage those who consider our mountain to be their own personal bully pulpit to keep in mind that freedom of expression, like our lovely forests, is a God-given privilege. Let us not abuse it."

"Yeah, self-abuse should suffice," said Sam.

HALFWAY THROUGH FOOTBALL PRACTICE ON MONDAY, with Lucy and her girls watching from the hillside, Bruno huddled with Ward for a minute before Ward called us all together.

"We're cutting off early because we have the extra week," he said. "This is the last series of the day. Four downs, starting from midfield. If the offense gets a first down, they get tomorrow off. If the defense stops them, tomorrow's a holiday for the D. Lefferts, you're in for Bannion."

Two runs by Addison and Anthony gained nothing. Madden called a slant for Will on third down, but Zowitzki tipped it away.

"I want this mother," Madden said in the huddle. "I could use a day off. I need ten yards. Martin, what do you want to run?"

"I got the play," I heard myself say.

Faces turn toward me in disbelief.

"Vic, listen," I said. I think it was the first time I'd ever called him by his first name. "Thorn is crowding the line. He wants to take my head off. I can beat him long. They'll be all over Martin."

"Forget it," said the quarterback. "Bomb's low percentage. Martin, run an out."

Will shook his head. "He's right. Zowitzki's going to try and mug me. Let him do it."

Madden stared at Will. Will stared back. Then Madden stared at me. "All right, Martin runs a slant. Lefferts, I'll pump-fake you on an out, then you turn up." He paused. He'd lost face to Will. He wasn't about to lose face to me. "You'd better leave his ass in the grass."

"I will," I said.

I faked the squareout, but Thorn didn't bite: he'd figured it out. He was by my side as we sprinted together, flat out.

'Roids versus the Reservoir. We were running so fast that when I looked back over my shoulder, Madden's pass was actually a little short. I had to come back for it. I leapt straight up. Meantime, Thorn wasn't playing the ball: he was timing his hit, trying to kill me. And it was a good hit: as I jumped, his helmet bludgeoned my left thigh. But while my brain cringed at the pain, my hands thought for themselves: they caught the ball.

I went flying, and landed hard on my right shoulder. Then I popped up and flipped the ball to Thorn, just to mock the guy. He swatted it about twenty yards, supremely pissed off.

Clune gave me a congratulatory head-butt. "Day off! Yeah!"

Madden? No smile. But a nod. Good enough.

• • •

When I saw Lucy waiting outside the locker-room door after I'd showered and changed, I figured she was waiting for the quarterback. "He's getting ultrasound on his ankle," I told her.

"Where you headed?" she said. "Can I walk with you?"

I shrugged my shoulders. If I got caught up in this web, all the good stuff that was happening could fall apart. My head was saying no. Something else was going along with her.

"That was a pretty cool catch," she said. "Thorn was trying to kill you."

"Just somebody else who wants to turns me into meat," I said.

"That's what your sport is all about, right?" she said. "Who can outdick the other guy?" I didn't say anything, even if she'd nailed it. "So are you and me ever going to hang together, or not?"

They were ten of the longest seconds I've ever lived.

"Probably not," I said.

In the back of my head I saw a curtain falling on something. Or like I'd just closed a door made of lead.

Maybe I was stupid, but I was goddamned *smart* too. And that seemed to be happening a lot lately.

But *damn,* I thought, as she tossed that ponytail and walked away. For the last time. Which felt shitty. And somehow, at the same time, good. Like I'd won a game.

THE LOCKER ROOM SEEMED QUIETER THAN usual. Something was up. Ward walked over to me. "Lefferts," he said, staring at his clipboard, "you're down with the JVs today."

What?

"They need bodies down there, and we got Saturday off, so you get an extra game."

"Come on, Mr. Ward," I said. "What's the *real* deal?" I looked over at Madden's locker, but the captain wasn't there. Could Madden be that powerful? I take a ten-yard walk with his Muffy, and now I'm minor league?

"The deal is what I said it is, Lefferts. Mr. Jarvis needs a receiver. His QB is out, he has to go with the backup. You could use the work." He looked up from his clipboard. "And you have a pretty big ego for a kid who's caught, what, two passes? So get down to the pond—ten minutes ago."

I banged the side of my locker with my fist: stupid. I could have bruised the hand. As if my "talented" hands were doing me any good anyway.

"Hey, cool out." It was Will. "Don't give them a reason to

make it permanent. Look at the bright side. You'll probably get a lot of catches."

He was right. Plus, I got Jarvis instead of Ward, and that was a trade I could live with. I jogged down to the pond. Pick your battles to win the war, right?

Jarvis was waiting for me at the bottom of the path, and the rest of the JVs were stretching. "Pearson threw out his elbow in some game of touch," Jarvis said. "And hey, I like to win as much as the next guy. So all I got is Alex at quarterback. Ward offered you up after the faculty meeting last night." He chewed on a knuckle. "So do me the favor. Bury the pride. I'll bump up your grade."

Actually, it was kind of nice to be back on the pond. Alex jogged over. His helmet was jiggling like a bobblehead doll.

"Hey, this is gonna be great. Oh, man, this is gonna be so great," he said.

The kid who covered me in the practice was a tenth grader—small, but tough. He hit hard, but he couldn't keep up with my moves, and Alex was throwing good spirals. No pressure. Just ball.

On the final play of the practice, I caught a long pass and sprinted sixty yards into the end zone, into the wind coming off the pond. I could smell the flavor of fresh water when it starts getting colder. Soon, there'd be ice forming on the fringes, the earth beginning to lock up and turn toward winter.

I used to see it on the Reservoir. Up here, I thought, it was going to be the real thing: Winter coming in. Getting warm by a fireplace. Maybe with a . . . friend.

That night, in the practice room, with no weed and no wine, The Others were musicians, pure and simple. We were beginning to rehearse now: we had something we'd composed, something original, to break down, tweak, caress. The second time through, I looked up from the piano. Simon was drumming with his eyes closed. Josh was grinning at me. Danny was just nodding with each bass note, losing himself, as we all were—in the soft parts, in the storms, in the highs and the lows.

Then the echoes of the final notes whispered away into the silence of the room.

"We *wrote* that?" said Simon. "Geez."

"So what are we going to call it?" Danny said.

What would a song by The Others be called?

"'Everything Else,'" I said.

"Cool," said Simon, nodding. "We play the stuff you don't hear anywhere else. So now, what do we do with it?"

"The holy Thanksgiving concert," I said.

"No way," said Simon. "That's all classical. Scouts from Sony. The admin in tuxes. Alt stuff need not apply. Besides, you're supposed to be the First Piano that night, not the indie keyboard player."

"No way," I said, and as I said it, I finally knew it was

true. I was bowing out of the competition. Thank fucking God. "I dropped out of that game."

They all looked at me.

"Seriously?" said Danny.

"Seriously," I said, which sealed the deal. I could tell the bond among us had just grown a little stronger.

"I like it—we make a little Oakhurst Hall history," Danny said. "New tradition."

"And we're going to do this *how?*" said Simon.

"Our only chance to even *get* a chance is to have a wingman," said Josh. "Faculty adviser. What about Jarvis, Jack?"

"No good," said Danny. "The head thinks he's nuts."

"Yeah. We need a heavyweight," Josh said. "Someone Carlton listens to."

"What about McGregor?" I said.

"Corporate McGregor?" Josh said. "Are you crazy?"

"Why not?" I said. "He used to be a musician. He's on Carlton's team."

Simon laughed. "What do we have to lose? We've already been admitted to this place. The dude can't unadmit us."

As the band packed up, I told them I was going to stay back, practice for my next lesson. When they'd left, I walked down the hall toward the chords that were shaking the whole damned building. Amazing. Like the soundtrack for a marching army a hundred years ago. Definitely Russian.

I opened the door, and there he was, as I knew he'd be. He stopped playing. "You practicing for the audition? You got your piece?"

"Come on," I said. "You know it was the band rehearsing. And you gotta admit, Mario, we're getting there. We're not half bad."

"It's nice," he said. "I'll give you that. Definitely original. And don't think I can't hear the Schubert in there."

"So anyway," I said. "About the big night. It's yours. I'm out."

He pushed away from the piano. Then he slumped his head; I couldn't tell if he was happy or bummed. When he looked up I could tell that it was both. "Why?"

"Well, for one thing, I wouldn't stand a chance. You know it, and I know it. Come on—you were just playing, what?"

"Prokofiev. Soundtrack to *Aleksandr Nevsky*. Was it any good? I can never tell."

"Mario," I said, "it was amazing. No way we're going to leave this year to Hopper the head case."

He stood up and stuck out his hand. We shook. "It's going to make my parents pretty happy, that's for sure. But I wish I'd earned it."

"Oh, you earned it," I said. "Trust me."

As I turned to leave he said, "I owe you."

"Comrade," I said, "the only thing you owe me is to play your ass off on the big night. Otherwise, you're going to hear it from me. So what are you going to play?"

"The Rach 3, I guess."

Right. Only the hardest freaking piano concerto ever written.

Down at the pond on Saturday afternoon, I looked around at the tiny crowd: a dozen parents on the home sideline, a half dozen parents from a private middle school down in Massachusetts who'd made the drive up to see their ninth graders try and knock off the big preppie JVs—and a girl in a big, shapeless hoodie standing over near the pond watching a few dozen Canada geese who'd just lifted off from the pond.

She turned around. She was smiling a smile that was a lot wider than her usual shy smile, which meant that she knew how happy I'd be that she'd surprised me. And she was right.

I left the warm-ups and jogged over. "I went looking for you, and Josh told me you were back with the JVs," she said. "I thought you could use some moral support."

"Yeah," I said. "I'm going back to my humble roots."

"You'll do great. Maybe you'll even have fun. Maybe today you can leave the trail."

Without thinking, I reached out a hand. She put hers in mine. Then took it back.

"I have to get back up there," she said. "We have a meet in an hour. Booth'll kill me if I'm late."

She jogged away. I watched her bounce up the path.

"Jack!" I heard Jarvis shout. "Get over here!" I turned around to see our guys lining up to receive the opening kick-off and hustled back to our sideline.

"Okay," Alex said in the first huddle. "I'm gonna hit Lefferts on a bomb. Everyone hold your blocks. Gimme time to throw it. You got it?" Nine helmets bobbed in unison.

The defender faced me across the line. I broke downfield like a sprinter. But the guy stayed with me stride for stride and just when I expected the ball to land in my lap, he reached in and batted it away. Great play. This wasn't going to be as easy as I thought. As I watched the ball bounce away, I knew in a flash: I'd gotten a little too cocky.

"Same play," Alex said in the huddle, all business. Then he looked me in the eye. "Like the touch game."

"Come on, Alex," said one of the other kids. "He's had one practice with us."

"Same play," said Alex.

"Pump-fake me on a square out," I said. "Then I'll go long."

He nodded his bobblehead. We lined up. At the snap, I took off, cut sharp right, felt the cornerback move in to try for the interception, then took off upfield. Alex's pass nestled into my hands, and I outran the rest of them: my first touchdown for Oakhurst, Well, sort of. But it felt good anyway.

As I trotted back to the bench, I saw a big blue bird take off from the water with two huge slow-motion flaps of its wings and bank off toward some pine trees.

"Jack," I heard Jarvis say, "you with us, or the heron?" The Zen master was still a coach. I had to do him right. So on the next series, when Alex drilled a slant a few feet behind me, I pictured the ball hitting my hands, reached behind, snagged it, and ran about forty yards diagonally through their defensive backfield . . . until, when I slowed up, like a showboating idiot, a guy dragged me down from behind on the five-yard line.

"That's your mulligan," said Jarvis, rightfully angry. "Ward would want your head on a platter. Try taking the game seriously, Jack. You might learn something."

The words hit home. On the next series I took a short pass, headed upfield, dodged one tackle and then another, and when their safety wrapped an arm around my waist, I shifted my hip, and he fell away. The whole thing was kind of like a blur. All I knew was that my instincts were kicking in. I was a split second ahead of everyone. This must be the difference between college and the pros, I thought. I was a pro.

I reached the end zone and politely handed the ball to the official.

It was 21–0 at the half. Alex walked over and said, "Hey,

Jarvis told me to stop throwing to you 'cause they don't want to embarrass these guys 'cause it isn't good sportsmanship."

I spent the rest of the game teaching myself more about how to play football: mainly, blocking defenders, running really precise roots, losing the ego. Since I knew that I wasn't going to have to do anything else, I laid a hit on anyone I could find—high, low, and in between. I blocked the cornerback. I blocked the linebacker. I blocked a lineman from behind, just for the hell of it, and got a penalty. I blocked two guys so that Alex could score on a bootleg.

We won, 42–14. When it was over, I traded high fives, low fives and fist-bumps with a bunch of kids I didn't know, and the one I did. Then I accepted a firm handshake from Jarvis.

"Now do it up next week for Bruno," he said.

As I walked off the field, I saw Clune waiting for me, after the varsity practice.

"I heard you ate 'em up the first half," he said.

"Yeah, it was pretty cool," I said.

He walked with me up the path. "You're gonna be a star next year, man. Zowitzki, Mancini, they'll be gone. Pearson's got a good arm. Bruno'll shut Ward up and take over for real. You'll be raking 'em in."

"If Thorn hasn't taken out my knees by then," I said. And suddenly it felt like a good time to find out what I had to know. "Mike, break this down for me. Who's on, and who's off? The juice?"

He stopped, looked around, waited for the last cluster of JVs to walk by us. Then we started walking, slowly. "For Christ's sake, you didn't get this from me, okay?" I nodded, "Zowitzki, Thorn, Mancini do the needles. Three or four other guys on defense do every supplement you can find from every sleazy website from here to Japan, but they stay away from the needles."

"What about offense? Madden?"

"Clean. Doesn't need it, with his arm. Leaves the juice to Anabolic Addison and the left side of the line . . . the guys he needs to protect him. And Bannion, believe it or not. Just to make Vic like him. He also thinks it makes him a stronger kicker. And he still sucks.

"The champ is Swicky. He'll shoot up anything his dealer ships him. He's nuts. And I mean that seriously. The juice works in mysterious ways, and not all of them are good. Take my word on that."

"So you too?" I said, my heart sort of sinking. We'd reached the varsity field now. It was empty, but the light towers were still looming like sci-fi monsters, and I was seeing the field in a new kind of way.

"Not since fourth form—two years ago," he said. "I weighed two sixty. I was having an all-America season until I pulled about forty muscles I never knew I had. Now it's just the vitamins. Fred Flintstone never needed 'roids."

· · ·

Corporate McGregor looked up from his desk. The fire was crackling. His tie was still yellow. He must have had a dozen yellow ties. "Jack! Come on in. How's it going? How's that audition piece? Going to give Mario a run for his money?"

"Actually, sir, no," I said. "I'm not going to compete this year."

McGregor frowned. "Why not?"

"You know—commitments and stuff. Grades. Football and . . . music. That's actually why I'm here. Like I told you, the band, we're writing this . . . I don't really know what you'd call it, a song, only it's about fifteen minutes long. It's kind of modern."

He nodded. "That's, well, terrific. This is for an elective?"

"Not really," I said. "It's just on our own. Anyway. We think the song is pretty good, and we were thinking of maybe trying to perform it at the Thanksgiving concert."

"*Real*-ly," he said, like I'd suggested that he quit his job and join a carnival. "Have you talked to the head about this? That concert is purely classical, as I'm sure you know. Perhaps in the winter, or next year, we could plan for . . . an evening for the student groups. A sort of battle of the bands!"

I'd figured that it was going to be hopeless. But I couldn't back down now. "Sir, it's not about competing. We sort of thought that if we made that night about *all* kinds of music, not just classical, it would mean more to the whole school. To the kids. It's their school, right?"

"Well, Oakhurst Hall is *all* of us, Jack. Not just the students, but the alumni and all the people who have sacrificed so much for this institution."

"Right. Exactly. It's about pride in our school, sir. And if we join together . . . you know, as a community and all . . . well, I mean, we might have a better chance to perform it if we had a faculty adviser for the group."

He was already only half listening. I saw him sneak a glance at some forms on his desk. Application forms. Finding the next rich future alum. "That'd probably be a good start. Have you asked Mr. Hopper?"

"I was thinking more that maybe you could do it, sir."

"Me?"

I couldn't believe he hadn't seen it coming. "Well, remember last year when I talked to you the first time?" I said. "You probably don't, but you said you liked music? All you'd have to do is come listen to us, and maybe you'd like it." But this was so off his radar he didn't know what to say. He tried to look like he was in control while he came up with an answer.

"Well, I don't . . . that is, my duties here are very specific. I've never . . . and I'm awfully busy . . . but I do appreciate your thinking of me."

"Sure, I understand," I said. "No big deal." I stood up.

"Thanks for your time, Mr. McGregor," I was almost out the door when he said, "Jack."

I turned around. He'd stood up. "I"ll try and make a rehearsal. Keep me posted."

"Will do," I said. "I'll shoot you an e-mail."

"That'd be fine," he said, sitting back down to look at his applications. "Jill might enjoy it. My wife is quite the character," he said, without looking up.

"I'm sure she would, sir," I said. "Maybe you would too."

"GET YOUR HEAD ON STRAIGHT, LEFFERTS." Ward's head was buried in his clipboard. "Just 'cause you scored a few TDs against fifth graders doesn't mean we're impressed."

"Mr. Ward," I said, "my head has been on straight from the first day of practice. Just give my hands a few chances."

He raised his head and looked me square in the eye. "You'll get your chances. Now get your ass down to the field."

But in practice, Madden didn't throw me a single pass. Then Ward made me run two laps for standing on the sideline without my helmet on—even though that wasn't even a rule, as far as I knew.

Then Thorn clotheslined me on one pattern and hit my windpipe so hard I couldn't breathe for about ten seconds. He laughed. "'Revenge is a dish best served cold!'" he said. "*Star Trek: The Wrath of Khan*!" It was like something Sam would have said. Weirdly, he reached out an arm to help me up.

Weirder still, I took it. He was a teammate.

But I was getting real tired of their game, which is what I told Will as we hiked up to the locker room. "Time to grow up and face the music," he said. "It's a goon squad, and for better or worse, you're part of it now. The good thing is that Thorn and Zowitzki play for us. Trust me, we're not the only team that couldn't pass a piss test."

"Essex?" I said.

"Loaded," he said. "We're gonna need your band up on the hill again." He looked over at me. "So when do we get to hear this thing you guys are cooking up?"

I told him about McGregor and the Thanksgiving concert. And how I wanted to get The Others onto that stage that night.

"I like it," he said, nodding. "Anything I can do, let me know."

"Okay, sure," I said. "What can you do?"

Will laughed, shaking his head. "Dude, I'm the Hall's dream: a multi-cultural kid with an army dad and a European mom. My SAT scores are off the charts, and I already got an off-the-record early admission offer for a full ride at Dartmouth. I can get away with anything around here." He grinned. "Although getting your band onstage at Thanksgiving might be pushing it."

Hopper didn't say anything when I came in for the next lesson. His vibe was neutral. He'd had his say, I'd had mine. The time had come for us to figure out where we were going.

I spread the sheet music out for the second allegro, and

began to play. It was probably going to be easier to talk to him with music. He turned around to look at me when he heard the first few measures. So I stopped playing. "Mr. Hopper," I said, "I'm not going to compete for First Piano."

He'd expected it, and I could tell he'd rehearsed it when he launched into his comeback. Every word sounded like a knife chop. "Your action is an insult. I have not only considered you worthy, I've contributed to your growth."

And in a way, he had. I couldn't really connect the dots, but whatever had happened in this practice room had made me a better keyboard for the band—if only because I some-how knew I never wanted to turn out to be a Hopper.

"Sir," I said, "I'm not cut out to be a picture in a hall-way. I don't want to be a picture in any hallway. I want to be a picture on a CD—with Josh and Danny and Simon."

I didn't think he heard a word.

"This is unprecedented," he said. "I've never had a student voluntarily decline to perform for the First Piano compe-tition. And I do not enjoy feeling as if my talent is being wasted." I swear I saw his eyebrows grow a half inch longer.

"Excuse me, sir," I said, "but I thought you enjoyed making me a better piano player. Which you have. You really have. I mean, I know I came in here with an attitude. But our band . . . I wish you'd hear us, sir. When I play this thing we've written, I really do . . . articulate."

Maybe it was the last word that got through, because he

looked me in the eye, then ambled over to his cluttered desk and slumped into his chair. It was almost a little sad. Almost. But he was suddenly a completely different guy.

"Jack," he said, "you have a gift. I can now see that you feel the emotion behind the notes. And very few pianists have come into this room over the last few years who can feel them like that. Who know that every note was written because it carried an emotion." Then he sifted through some old sheet music and tugged at his tie. "Fewer of them every year. Oh, they're technical wizards. They have perfect pitch. But they have no heart."

He looked up at me. I'm not sure he was seeing me. Then he shuffled some more sheet music. "Perhaps we're admitting a different kind of student these days. They seem more . . . driven to succeed. And so my job is to not only teach them, but to . . . drive them. Whip them. They're the thoroughbreds, I suppose. But that's my job, Jack. My job is to get them to win their races."

"So aren't there some fast horses," I said, "that would just rather run wild?"

Hopper's caterpillar eyebrows arched. When he said, "*Are* there any wild horses anymore, Jack?" we were on the same page, for the first time.

"I read about some on an island off the shore of Maryland," I said. It was in one of Simon's magazines. We'd finally found a common ground. Hopper had stepped down from his platform, and I'd stopped playing the stupid rebel in the face of a man who really did know what he was doing. Even if he was layered in Oakhurst Hall lacquer.

I wondered for the first time, was he a dad? Did he have kids who'd disappointed him?

"And sir," I said, "come on, you have to admit—there's Mario, and then there's the rest of the world."

Hopper nodded, giving up. "He has talent. But he'll never be able to represent Oakhurst Hall in the real world— the world that matters. Unfortunately, as of now, this year, he has no real competition."

"Yeah," I said. "But in a fair world, sir, he never did."

Hopper didn't answer. I'd hit home.

I quietly picked up my music and headed toward the door. I turned back to say something. I don't know what it would have been. But Hopper was looking out the window, with his hands clasped behind his back, and I figured maybe he wanted to do some thinking. I didn't want to get in the way right then.

I'd decided that I had another fence to mend. We had two games left. I needed a quarterback.

Madden had a corner locker twice as big as anyone else's. I approached him after practice the next day. In the locker he'd pinned up a shot of Peyton Manning when he was a Colt, a shot of his family, and a *Sports Illustrated* bikini poster of a girl who was supposed to look sexy, but you could tell was bored out of whatever was in her skull, if there was anything in her skull.

"Hey, Lefferts," he said, looking up with the same expression I'd seen all year, the one that judged you because of who you were and where you came from, and saw a gulf that wouldn't ever be crossed. "What's up?" He said it casually, as if we'd been talking to each other all season.

"How come you have it in for me? How come you have to be such a hard-ass all the time?"

"Because some of my guys are willing to make the sacrifice. And some don't care about the team."

His guys?

"That's bullshit," I said, "and you know it. It's not like it'd make me into a better receiver. I have the hands, I do the weights, and I got the motivation. But the needles? Nope. Plus, it's cheating, and you know it."

His laugh was heavy on the sarcasm. "Yeah, city boy, get all moral on me. Tell me what it's like to be honest when you come from bucks that pave your golden fucking future. You telling me that however the hell your family got the dollars that put you here were honest? They didn't cheat anyone? They didn't mess somebody over?"

I couldn't argue with him there. That was for sure.

Then he stood up, moved in a little closer and looked down at me. He was only about four inches taller, but suddenly I felt like a little kid. "Lemme tell you about 'morality.' My dad took out loans so I could come here and get an education. When he was in his twenties, he played semipro on weekends. He wanted me to have a chance."

Then he smiled this smile I'd never seen from him. Like I wasn't even there, The next thing he said was like he'd forgotten to have an attitude. "I swear to Christ, he always said it the same way: 'I want you to play a great sport the way it's meant to be played.'"

I wanted to tell him how much his dad sounded like mine, but then he was back at being Madden, and looking down at me, and preaching at me. "Only now I play in a league where Chelton and Williamton and Essex are taking fucking monkey hormones from Russia and trying to tear my knees apart. Which happen to be connected to my arm, which is all I got right now."

He peeled off his jersey, and turned to go to the showers. Then he stopped and looked back at me. "Lefferts, this game is all I got. And you're going to lecture me on cheating?"

All I could come up with was, "Hey, I'm just trying to be good at the game and maybe feel like a winner at something. Something that was *my* idea. That no one ever told me I had to do."

He looked at me completely neutrally. Like for the first time he was maybe taking me seriously, when, maybe, for the first time, I was taking him seriously, too. "And I'm trying to win a championship," he said, "with an undefeated season because, you know what? Ward says the day we play Essex, a scout from Ohio State is gonna be standing up on that frickin' hillside. Maybe even Michigan and Wisconsin. I'm scraping a C average here, but if I'm hot that day, maybe I get a free ride in a D-I program, where even if your team sucks, someone's filming it. And if I'm not good enough? Then maybe I get a degree that gets me a job with some alum. Either way, Dad's set. Get it?"

I heard him. Big time. But I'd started it, so I wasn't going to wimp out now. "So it's all about you? What happened to *team*?"

"Team? Team is when you win, man. That's what *team* is. You ever hear a bunch of losers in last place say, 'It doesn't matter, 'cause we were a team'? Only winners get to talk about how great it is to be on a 'team.' And to win, I need receivers."

"You got one," I said.

I walked back to my locker. Meatheads came in a lot of flavors. So did smart guys.

And Madden had me thinking. But he hadn't changed my mind.

AT BAND PRACTICE, TWO NEW SPECTATORS were sitting on the floor against the back wall.

"Practice ended early for the Almost-All-Asian Chamber Music Octet," Sam said. "We heard that you might need some support for your warped ambitions."

"We have been hearing bits of your very strange music from down the hall," Seo Woon said. "We had to see if up close it looks as weird as it sounds."

The band seemed happy enough to have an audience of any kind. Then, all of a sudden, we had more.

I'd been e-mailing McGregor about our practices whenever I knew we were going to practice, because we weren't getting high or drinking anymore, but I hadn't told the band, because he hadn't answered, and I figured he never would.

So when the door opened and McGregor walked in with his wife, everyone sort of froze.

His wife didn't look anything like I figured she would. She worked in the "development" office, which was a real subtle way of saying "the money-getting department," but she didn't look like a fund-raiser. She was pretty, but not in a prep way—a *real* way, with wrinkles, like someone who hadn't been afraid to jump the walls out into the real world. She had a long, brown ponytail, and her jeans were worn down to the last threads in the places your jeans are supposed to have holes: in the knees, in the butt. Like they'd been worn by someone with a life.

"This is so cool!" she said to her husband. "Music that's newer than the eighteenth century at Oakhurst Hall!"

"Jill was a big rock fan in the eighties," McGregor explained to the room.

She shrugged. "A few Bowie concerts," she said. "Lou Reed. Stuff like that."

"Well, all *right* then," Danny said. They sat in a couple of old chairs. "We call this Everything Else, a rock symphony in three movements."

Then I heard myself weigh in: "The first movement is called 'Hope.' The second is 'Chaos.' The third is called 'Calm.'" The whole band looked at me. I shrugged. We could work on that part later.

And then, exchanging crazy glances—*Can we do this?*—we laid it down: The smooth birdsong opening, with its wandering melodies; the crazy middle, veering into everything from Phish to the Foos; the peaceful conclusion, which had started to almost sound like the end of a Sunday-morning Carlton-sermon hymn, only without the downer vibe.

During the whole fifteen minutes, I watched McGregor

try to nod in rhythm, but he never quite got it right, although that wasn't really his fault, because the rhythm kept changing. I could tell that what we'd written wasn't for someone from the past. Just kids like us or like McGregor's wife. His own brain was telling him to remember that he represented a school and wore yellow ties with lacrosse sticks on them and he was married to some big money family and he couldn't risk muddying the waters if he was going to be Phil McGregor.

In the middle of the crazy second movement, when Josh and Danny were facing each other peeling crazy riffs, I knew that he wasn't going to back us. I also didn't care, because we were in the Zone.

His wife listened to the whole thing with her eyes closed, sometimes slapping the thigh of her jeans, in perfect time, and nodding.

When we finished, it was Jill McGregor who spoke first.

"Killer!" she said. "Wow. Too bad you guys weren't around with Lou Reed and the Velvets." McGregor coughed. Twice. "It's going to be a great Thanksgiving concert this year, guys," she said.

"Well, I'm sure it will be," said Corporate McGregor. "Whether these boys play their . . . song . . . or not. It was very impressive, Jack. Quite original . . . and, well, to write something like that, from scratch, well, that shows a lot of *enterprise*. Well, we'd better get going."

"Yep, I guess we'd better," his wife said, and left it at

that. As they walked out of the room, she turned back with a more serious look on her face. "Do not give up, guys. Okay? Promise?"

"Don't worry about that," Danny said.

The door slowly slid closed, leaving a hush like a morgue.

"So?" said Danny. "What're our chances with the man?"

"Less Than Zero," Sam said.

"Even with her bucks and connections?" said Josh.

"Face the music, son," answered Simon. "Carlton's not going to listen to a babe tell him what to do with his school, no matter how big her trust fund is. If she was really into rocking boats, you think she'd be married to McGregor? And trust me: Corporate man is rockin' no boats."

Sam and Seo Woon rose from the floor and headed for the door. "If you want my opinion," Sam said, "you could really use a Korean string section. Or some talent." Then they took each other's hands. Seo Woon looked at us. "That was . . . amazing," she said, as they walked out the door. "Good luck, guys."

For a few seconds, we just stood there. Then Josh put his guitar in its case and slammed it shut. Simon hit the snare so hard I thought he'd break the stick. Maybe it had been a mistake—*my* mistake—to try and take it seriously. I could feel their shoulders sagging all around me. Old Oak Hall would always find a way to beat you down.

Unless someone beat it back.

"I'm going to the top," I said.

"As in the Carlton top?" said Josh.

"What do we have to lose?" I said. "What can he say other than no?"

"Well, how about, 'Are you out of your mind, son?'"

"What's he going to do?" I said. "Use it against me that I have *enterprise*?"

"The name of a starship?" Simon said. "That has to be a good omen."

As if.

THE HEAD'S OFFICE WAS THE SIZE of basketball court. One wall to the side was mostly just a whole lot of little windows looking out onto the quad. His fireplace was as big as the one in the dining room. The desk reminded me of an aircraft carrier deck.

It was getting dark really early now, so that even though it was only late afternoon, the fireplace flames reflected in the glass of the framed diplomas hanging behind him.

The only other light was from the two amber desk lamps positioned at either side of him.

Pools of shadow gathered in the corners. A dark blue rug muffled my footsteps.

"Hello, Jack. Have a seat." Carlton didn't get up.

He was looking at a file in front of him. I sat in one of the two Oakhurst-crested wooden chairs facing his desk. "Looks like this might be our year on the football field, eh, son?" he said, not looking up. "Anglican will be tough next week, though. They're a very disciplined team. And, of course, Essex is quite the force this year."

"If you're busy, sir, I can wait," I said. "I know I'm a little early. If you have work—"

He looked up. "I'm just glancing at your file, Jack."

My file? I didn't know I had a file. "That's all about me?"

"Teacher reports, routine paperwork, the like," he said. "Grades—impressive, except for French. As for music . . . Mr. Hopper seems less than impressed."

"That's what I wanted to see you about, sir. Music."

"Yes. This band of yours—which took particular liberties at that football game, and quite illegally, I might add." Carlton closed the file and leaned back in his chair, giving me a serious look. "You know that the mountain is off-limits without faculty supervision."

"Sir, that wasn't—"

"Jack," he said, getting all head-y, "I understand that transition at *any* age of adolescence is difficult. You've arrived at Oakhurst Hall at an awkward stage, when most of your classmates have been here for two years and under-stand our customs. Our *traditions*."

Five heavy chapel chimes broke into the silence through the thick glass windows. Weirdly, somehow they sounded twice as loud in here. Like they were sealing my fate. I had this spacey flash that maybe he had them amplified into his office.

"But to take full advantage of the Oakhurst Hall experi-ence, you must accept that we are now your family. *In loco parentis,* as they say."

I knew that was Latin for "in the place of your parents." But right then? All I could think was, *All parents are loco.*

Now the head leaned forward, his eyes squinting at me, concerned. "Jack, do you think Oakhurst Hall and Jack Lefferts are a good fit?"

Wait a second. This meeting had been my idea. And now Carlton was reading to me from some perp sheet file? A voice in the back of my head told me to cool it. "I think I like it here, sir, if that's what you mean."

"That's fine," Carlton said. "But liking the school isn't enough, Jack. Being a part of the community means giving back to it. Admittance to Oakhurst Hall is a two-way contract."

Contract? I hadn't signed any contract. How was I supposed to answer that one? I let my eyes wander over to some pictures on the wall. A sailboat. Some dogs. Lots of shots of a Notre Dame college team. No new people. No women. All the old days.

"Well, I'm helping the football team," I said. That was a stretch.

"Football has been very good for you, Jack. But your decision to not compete for the First Piano position? Quite unheard of. Especially since, as I'm sure you know, one of the major factors in your admittance was your talent at the piano."

Ah. Got it. I mean I always figured that was the deal, but to hear it sort of sucked. Like I was a one-trick freak or something.

"And I'm sure that you know, by now, what the Thanksgiving concert means to everyone."

"I know what it means to Mario," I said.

He paused. Then he tried to sound casual. "Mario Miles is, of course, a very good musician. But the First Pianist has been known to enjoy exposure: not just on the ensuing tour, but farther down the road. This is a heavy mantle for some to carry. Especially if this year's concert is televised. Which could bring a great deal of welcome exposure to our institution."

As soon as he said it, I knew he wanted to take it back. Mario was good enough to play with the goddamned Boston Pops starting next Tuesday. But he wasn't good enough to represent a school that didn't have a clue what made the kid tick and didn't care, and only knew what his T-shirts said. It was all pretty clear now: Communists don't usually throw money back at the old school.

Carlton looked back down at the file and shuffled some papers. "Unfortunately, as things turned out this year, you and Mario seem to be far ahead of the rest of the pack. Now, we all need challenges to improve ourselves, Jack, and with your obvious skills, your 'band' hardly provides that challenge, do you think?"

"But it does, sir. It's the first time I've ever challenged myself." Then, luckily, Carlton's phone rang, because I needed some strategy here.

"Yes, that's fine," he said, and a second later, a maintenance guy came in with some firewood. "Thank you, Julio," Carlton said.

While the guy threw new logs on the fire, I checked out the titles of the books on the shelf. Lots of books about teaching and learning. A few Bibles. And one book called *Reaching Every Student*. That one triggered something. I didn't even wait until Julio had closed the door. I wanted to get the first word in.

"Sir, not every kid can win a prize, or get into Yale, or make Oakhurst Hall look better than all the other Oakhurst Halls," I said. "A lot of us aren't wired that way. Most of us never get that kind of a rush. But we all get a rush with music. Maybe it's heavy metal for the team or emo for Josh, but it's all the same language. To kids, music isn't a prize to win. It's the only thing we all share. Music is sort of the way our emotions sound out loud."

The new wood flared up, and I could see the reflection of the blaze in the window behind him. It was now completely dark outside.

"Rather like the emotion we feel on the hillside when Oakhurst scores a winning touchdown, yes?" Carlton said, reflexively glancing at the fire, like he was posing for a cover of the monthly school magazine. "The moment when an Oakhurst boy carries the ball into the end zone makes us all feel pretty proud, doesn't it?"

"But that's different!" I said, a little too loudly. "I mean, I can't wait until that's me. And I'm going to score that touchdown. I am. But what if our song made the school feel just as proud?"

His face dropped its magazine-cover cool; he was losing patience. "Well, Jack, this will be your first Thanksgiving concert, and, as I am sure you'll see, our symphony makes us *very* proud as a community, as we gather together—not on a hillside for a game, or in a chapel for camaraderie, but in an auditorium, to revel in the expertise of our artists."

The guy could preach. I had to give him that.

"And I think it's admirable of you to take the point position on this, as a new boy. But I can hardly seriously entertain the notion of your group playing at that concert. Bands are an extracurricular activity, as you well know. There are other forums for this kind of thing—the winter dance, for example."

"You can't really dance to the thing we've written, sir," I said. "It's sort of hard to describe. But I think it's something the students would really like to hear. I think it'd put them in a good place."

I guess that wasn't the right way to say it, because suddenly Carlton pushed his chair back scary quickly and shot to his feet. "A boy of sixteen hardly knows what place *he's* supposed to be in," he said, trying not to completely lose it. "And as for whatever *place* his peers want to be in? Right now, son, they are *here*. And I am their guide on the path to success."

He took a deep breath. I think he knew how spooky it was getting. "And when they are here, reaching them is my job. Not yours. I've made my decision. It is the right one. Am I clear about this, Mr. Lefferts?"

"Yes sir," I said. "Very clear."

But I'd made my own decision too.

In fact, I'd just made a very good one: We were going to play at the concert, one way or another. Carlton had just picked the wrong battle. We were going to win this war.

"I'm glad we had this talk, Jack," he said as he walked me to the door. "And good luck against Anglican." Suddenly, and oddly, he was smiling. "Let's give 'em hell!"

"Yessir!"

I think I might have actually said that. I might have even meant it.

As I walked out the door into the darkness, it was like being freed. And as I skipped down the stone stairs of the administration building, I knew that I could face the consequences of crashing the concert. If they booted me, they booted me. Because the me they'd be booting was a Jack Lefferts who'd learned how to play a sport with a team. To write a kick-ass song with another kind of team, maybe. A kid with a girlfriend in his future if he didn't mess it up. The kind of kid Oakhurst Hall needed more than it looked like Carlton would ever know.

Of course, the big question was how we were going to pull this off. Would Josh, Danny, and Simon really want to risk it? And how could we get the equipment onstage? And when?

I didn't want to show up Mario or the symphony. But we'd have to pull it off at the end—before Carlton and Ward and Booth and the SWAT team of Engleside, New Hampshire, could stop us.

MY *BACCHAE* PAPER WAS DUE THE next morning. As I walked to the library, two scenes flashed in my head: Jarvis's study and Carlton's office.

I stopped to look at the glass case with books by Oakhurst alums and photos of the authors. Two of them were by grads from the last twenty years: a woman who'd hit on a young adult theme involving paranormal romance and a guy who'd discovered lots of new fish in the Amazon. All the others were written by alumni from another age. There were pictures of them. All old and all white.

Instead of heading for a sleepy chair, I sat down in a cubicle, turned my computer on, and just wrote a story: about a school, somewhere long ago, where the headmaster was a king, living in a castle, and the kids ran into the woods to escape his rule. It was almost like writing a song. Whatever came into my head, I put it down.

In the end, the kids rebelled and burned the place down, then stood amid the ashes, wondering what in the hell to do next. Then they put it back together, only better.

I had no idea what Bruno would think, but at least it had come from me. It was mine.

Back in my room, I checked the internet window: open. I had four new e-mails: from Luke, from McGregor, from Jill McGregor, and from Caroline. Ten minutes ago.

I opened McGregor's first: *Jack—Thanks so much for asking me to hear your music. I wish I could give you better news, but my duties at Oakhurst Hall are clearly outlined and defined by my job description. To step outside of that box would set, at the very least, an unusual precedent. Jill and I wish you all the best in your endeavors.*

No surprise there.

Then I opened his wife's: *Dear Jack: Just wanted you to know that I thought your symphony was beautiful. Well, actually I thought it kicked, um, ass. And this is from an original Phish freak (I camped out at the Clifford Ball in Plattsburgh). I have passed my opinion of your music on to the powers that be. Good luck.*

Luke was the usual: *Jints lose to the goddamned Falcs cuz eli throws an INT to a fuckin DT? University is the yoozsual: tight-assed. No new babes. Want to go Iggles game over xmas break? Now that yr a futbal star?*

Caroline's words proved I'd saved the best for last. *Got best time on the team today! Miss you.*

I answered in a microsecond. *I miss you too.* To put it

mildly. Which took a lot of restraint. So I threw out the restraint. *Want to have a quick meet beneath the maple?*

It was about thirty seconds before she shot back, *See you in five.*

I whipped off an e-mail to my dad: *You coming up for the last game?*

I got an instant answer: *If I'm not there, a stretch Cayenne will be. Can't beat that, right?*

Right.

I was sitting beneath the tree when she came out dressed in a loose hoodie and, for the first time, a pair of really tight jeans that actually showed that she had a body. She flopped down next to me. "Any news on the band?"

"Not good. McGregor passed. And Carlton *really* shot me down. Like, in no uncertain terms. But I swear, we're going to play anyway."

"What if they boot you? How would I get through the rest of the year?"—and then she leaned her head on my shoulder, and right then, the band didn't matter. The history paper didn't matter. Ward and Carlton didn't matter. I did give a thought, though, to playing it cool as I slowly put my arm around her shoulder, then slid it down her side, then slipped it under the bottom of the sweatshirt—to feel nothing but soft skin. Her waist.

She didn't yank my hand away. So I just let it sit there.

The silken warmth of her skin felt unbelievably sexy. I lightly stroked it, that little patch of her stomach.

Neither of us said anything else for a few minutes. Then I turned my face to hers. She looked at me . . . smiled slyly, and hopped to her feet in one sudden, fluid motion. She looked down, smiled again, a little more slyly, and ran back up her dorm steps. If it was a tease, it was a tease I could live with.

I couldn't help seeing how naturally she ran, loping, like some forest animal, all in rhythm.

Of course, that wasn't all I noticed.

"GARVER, DO ME A FAVOR—LOSE YOURSELF for a second."
Zowitzki hovered in the aisle of the bus a few minutes
after we'd pulled away from campus. Heading to meet the
God Squad.

If we won, we'd be 5–0 going into the Essex game on
the last day of the term. Assuming Essex beat Williamton today, it would be a battle of the unbeatens. If we lost and they
won, the best we could hope for was a tie. On top of which,
it would make the concert a drag.

Anthony disappeared into the back of the bus. Zowitzki
slid into the empty seat. The linebacker didn't look at me,
just kept his pin-eyes on the movie: *We Are Marshall.* His right
knee was jackhammering up and down.

"Dude, listen, I know you're not gonna come around.
You been cool with the lifting. And cool that you told Lucy
to fuck herself. Madden appreciates that."

"No prob there. I think I found my girl."

"You're lucky. Anyway. Just so you know, now that we're
close to maybe winning it all, I figure, bygones, all that shit."

"Bygones," I said. "And all that shit. History. Cool."

Something was off with our Tasmanian Devil. His face had lost all the tension as he watched Matthew McConaughey up on the screen. "Took an MRI for my knee and my shoulder . . . they say there's some spot on my fucking liver or something. Maybe just a shadow on some bad film. Doctors here are numb-nuts anyway."

Fuck.

"Maybe it's nothing. You'll deal with it," I said, surprising myself. I really wanted him to. I was scared for him. "It'll be history."

He nodded, real fast, and popped to his feet like a jack-in-the-box. "Let's just make a little more history for a few more weeks on the field, okay? Then you and Mario can have your revolution."

"And you can have your ring."

He laughed—a fairly human laugh. Now he actually looked me in the eye.

"Cool," he said. "How you feeling?"

"I'm ready," I said. And I was.

Then he was Swicky again. He'd flicked a switch back to Neanderthal. He laughed his demonic giggle. "Me too. Gonna lay some hits today. Gonna rattle some Anglo brains."

Ward had tried to warn us against a letup, but Anglican was a weak team—their only win had come against Hesford. We were expected to coast. Anglican's thing was turning out Christians, not cretins.

"You might even catch a pass," Zowitzki said, disappearing down the aisle. Couldn't help himself.

As the bus pulled into the Anglican driveway, the parking lots were full. For Anglican, this was the final home game. The grandstand was packed. On our side, a busload of Oakhurst Hall kids had come up to cheer for the undefeated team.

We won the toss. I saw Bruno drawing on Ward's clipboard with a pencil, and Ward was nodding. Then he called us together. My attention wandered to the Oakhurst Hall kids. The only one I recognized was Lucy, who was with some of her posse. I had to admit, she was still hot as hell.

Suddenly I felt an elbow in my ribs. It was Will: "You listening to this, asshole?"

I zoned back into Ward's words.

". . . but we've never practiced it. It's a flanker screen. Listen up, Lefferts! Do I have your attention? Again, we're opening with two wideouts, and you as flanker right, in the slot. That oughta mess them up. If we can score on the first drive, they might roll over."

Flanker. Me.

"So this is the play. Lefferts, you line up inside Martin on the right, two steps behind him. Bannion splits left. At the snap, Lefferts, just stand there. Madden will get it to you, quick. Let's see some of that speed you're supposedly famous for. Martin will take out the cornerback."

The adrenaline was double-pumping. I lowered the helmet, slowly, trying to cool out. Snapped the chin strap. I could hear the blood pulsing in my ears.

I heard Will say, "Clune, you got that outside linebacker, right?"

"That's just the start. After that"—and Clune turned to me—"take it all the way, little guy."

Anthony returned the kickoff to the thirty-eight. In the huddle, Madden said, "You heard it. Flanker screen. On a quick-snap, got it? Hit your blocks. Make 'em stick. Give me time to get it out there to him."

As I trotted to my position, I wondered for a second whether this wasn't just another trick play—trick on me. If it was, they were going to a lot of trouble to sell it, though.

I could tell that the Anglican defense was confused. They'd never seen a three-receiver set. One of their linebackers was shouting out, "Hey, hey, get someone on eighty-eight . . ." just as Madden took the snap. Will fired out to the right, and the cornerback went with him.

To my left, Clune had already pancaked the outside backer, and now he was heading for the middle guy. I turned just in time to see the pass coming at me, but I was so pumped to get downfield, I took my eye off it. Madden's bullet bounced off my palms, straight up into the air, in slow motion, end over end.

Two and a half months . . . to get here . . . and blow it?

But while my head was thinking, my hands were taking over. They snatched the ball out of the air.

I cradled it, turned upfield.

And saw nothing but daylight.

Afterward, when I tried to piece the play together, trying to save it for my memory, all I remembered was a blur of bodies, different colors, shouts echoing just behind me, maybe a swipe or two, someone trying to grab my hip, my jersey, but always a little too late.

As I crossed the Anglican thirty, my senses were in overdrive: the sound of my cleats crunching into the grass, the smell of autumn, and the thuds of the stampede, now all behind me.

But I wasn't free yet. Out of the corner of my eye, the safety was closing in.

I shifted into Reservoir gear. He'd misjudged the angle and my speed. As I hit the ten-yard line, he dove at my ankles, and I could feel his hands clawing at my feet. I kicked back hard and high with my cleats on the next two strides, and he fell away.

I crossed the goal line—and ran right through the end zone, just to make sure. I wanted to jump thirty feet in the air. I wanted to spike the ball and scream at the top of my lungs.

Instead I just sort of stood there stupidly. I didn't

know how to act like I'd been there . . . because I'd never been there—until now.

And then Will was sweeping me up in a bear hug from behind, before dropping me to the ground.

"Feels pretty good, doesn't it?" the big kid said as we trotted back to the sideline.

And yeah, I was clutching the ball under my arm, protecting it like it was the crown jewels.

Back at the bench, a ton of hands slapped my pads—Clune, Anthony, even Zowitzki and Addison. Madden nodded at me. Not a half nod, but the nod of a teammate.

The quick strike set the tone. Madden was sharp after that. Loose. Will caught two bombs for TDs, and Addison took a screen all the way. I caught a slant, broke a tackle, and took it for fifteen. At halftime, the score was 21–7.

In the second half, I caught two more passes and laid down some vicious blocks. For the first time, I was starting to get that high that Clune had talked about when you meet a guy head-on, like maybe two rams butting heads—and you want it more. Like it was something tribal. The weights had done their work: there was something solid inside me now.

On one play in the third quarter, Ward actually lined me up wide to the right, where I was the only receiver, and called for another bomb. They rushed an extra guy over to cover me: sort of the ultimate compliment. Maybe in my whole life.

Seeing the coverage, Madden play-faked to Anthony up the middle, looked toward me and the double-coverage, then saw that Anthony was drifting around, open, and flipped the ball to him, just a short outlet pass—but my friend went straight down the field for thirty-five yards. Addison bulled it in for the final TD: 35–7.

We were one game from a perfect season.

With the final whistle, Zowitzki walked over and looked me in the eyes with that pinball stare. "Glad to have you on my team, Lefferts."

"Glad to be here," I said. "Like I told you. I just wanted to play football."

"You did today, dude."

I worked my way down the bus, slapping random palms stuck out into the aisle, and sank into my seat just as Bruno appeared in the aisle and flipped me the football from my touchdown. He'd put it aside. "You don't want to forget this." Then he walked back up to the front of the bus.

"You'll be the stud next season," Anthony said.

That was a very weird thought. Another season. Oakhurst Hall all over again?

Now Anthony peeled off to head for the back of the bus, where Mancini's speakers were blasting Eminem and the defensive linemen were dancing in the aisle. I sat back, still taking it all in. I turned the ball over and over in my hand, feeling the soft touch of the pigskin. I closed my eyes to replay the tape of the touchdown in my head.

Then the seat suddenly sank and Clune stuck out a

meaty hand. "That was a keeper. That's highlight-reel stuff. One more to go. But Essex is gonna be intense," he said. "My family's been waiting four years for this. Hell, half of Dorchester's gonna be there. Your family coming?"

"I don't think so," I said. "My dad has to be in Kansas or something. But it's cool."

"Not even if you play First Piano that night?"

I told him about dropping out of the competition.

"No shit? You're handing it to Mario?"

"I still might play, though. We might. The band."

Clune laughed. "And how you gonna work that?"

"I don't know yet," I said. "The head shot it down. Mc-Gregor shot it down. Breaks every rule in the book. So if we do, it's, like, against direct orders. But I want to try it anyway. What the hell, right?"

Clune whistled. "Little man, you got a big pair." He laughed, and we fist-bumped. "It'd beat the hell out of Beethoven. Give old Oak a kick in the ass. What do you think they'd do to you?"

I didn't want to think about that part. "First we'd have to figure out how to get the amps, the drums, the mikes on-stage and plugged in in, like, ten seconds."

Clune nodded. "Leave that to me. You do your part. I could do mine."

"Clune," I said, "I can't ask you to do that. You could get in some serious trouble."

"You didn't ask," Clune said. "I offered. What'll they do? Demerits? No one gets booted for carrying amps. Keep me posted, eighty-eight." And with that, Clune bobbed up off his seat and disappeared to the back of the bus.

If Will helped, that'd make two. This could actually work.

"Listen up!" Ward was standing in the aisle at the front of the bus. The movie screens went black. He waited until everyone quieted. Eminem went silent.

"One to go. And by the way—Essex beat Williamton by three touchdowns today. From now until next Saturday, all you think about is Essex. You are one game from immortality, gentlemen. One game from that golden trophy in the case. Listen up. Let's talk Essex."

The Green—that's what they called our rival—was good this year. Then, the Green was good every year. A big school in western Massachusetts that sent every other kid to Hah-vahd, Essex had it all: a good defense, a coach with twenty years under his belt who wasn't afraid to break out of the mold. Using a phenom Prep for Prep QB out of the South Side of Chicago, they ran a college-spread-option offense which we hadn't seen.

"They win with the QB—Carson. Period. He runs, he passes, he pitches it out. He scored every one of their TDs today. He's fast, he's smart, and the only way to keep him from killing us is a spy. So Zowitzki, you're gonna shadow him. Every play. Forget everything else. Where he goes, you go. He doesn't try to pick his nose without you grabbing his hand. You aim for the head. Take out the head, the body will die. I'll take fifteen lost yards over fifteen lost IQ points any day, any play."

"How much money if he leaves on a stretcher?" said Zowitzki.

"I give you extra props in my rec letter to that football factory in Alabama. But you're not in the NFL yet."

Then he told us about Essex's Zowitzki—a linebacker named O'Doul, already committed to Notre Dame. The kid was supposedly a monster, sideline to sideline—"Like Swicky, only not as ugly." That got some laughs. "He blitzes half the time. That means the backs gotta stay in to pick him up. That means you gotta get rid of the ball early, Madden. All right. That's it. Think Green. Think Dead Green."

"Dead Green!" Zowitzki shouted, and the team picked up on it: "Dead Green! Dead Green!"

The roar rocked the bus. I joined in. I wasn't faking it.

BRUNO WAVED A PAPER IN THE air. "Now, this is what I had in mind. *This* . . . is what I was talking about. This is history . . . but alive." I looked over at Lucy, figuring it was hers. It took me a second to focus, to hear Bruno read a few paragraphs from a story about Oakhurst Hall, and King Carlton, and some rebel kids fighting the system.

"Whose was it, Mr. Bruno?" said Thorn.

"Not yours," said Bruno, dropping it on my desk—with its big, red, circled A shouting out at me.

I'd never expected it. I'd expected a C, and I didn't care. But a real teacher giving a good grade to a gonzo fairy tale? Maybe the Gothic castle was growing me up. Just not in the way it thought it was going to.

We had a bigger audience at the next band practice: not just Sam and Seo Woon, but Caroline. They'd all just had symphony rehearsal. I'd only asked her to sit in about five times. We did the piece, and it could have been better, because this time I was trying to show off on the piano, when by now we all knew that the only way it worked was if no one tried to outshine anyone else. Even Josh's solos had started sounding more disciplined: less like Hendrix and more like Clapton.

After the final note faded away, everyone sat in silence for a good ten seconds before Caroline said, "You know, it really is good, guys. Like, beautiful."

"It *is* a symphony," Seo Woon said. "It's original. So when does the school get to hear it?"

"Carlton doesn't like it," Josh said. "He won't let us play at the Thanksgiving concert. So we're going to play it anyway." Simon laughed the crazy Simon laugh and whacked Danny in the butt with his sticks.

And so that was that. There was no going back. Everyone was on board.

Then Simon hit his tom-tom with both sticks, laid down a snatch from the "Wipe Out" drum solo. "All *right!*"

"Uh-*huh,*" said Danny, nodding, playing a cool, quick bass riff. "That's what I'm talking about. A little guerrilla action."

"We could catch a serious shitstorm for this," I said.

Simon shrugged. "What do we have to lose?"

"Other than your place in school?" said Sam. "And no Yale, and no Harvard Business, and no First Boston, and then no possibility of eventually ruling the global economy? Nothing."

"Come on," said Caroline. "Do you think Carlton would

kick out some kids who wanted to play music so badly they broke a few rules?"

"We'd shake the whole freakin' foundation," said Danny. "But what a way to go, huh?"

"Now," Josh said, "all you have to tell me is how we pull this off."

I'd been doing a lot of fast thinking lately. But it had been working out. "Okay," I said, making it up as I went along. "As soon as Mario finishes his final notes, and he's getting the standing O from everyone but Hopper and Carlton, we get the amps and drums on, kick the song off before people leave their seats."

"And we do that how, exactly?" Danny asked.

"As Joe Cocker put it at Woodstock," I said, "'We get by with a little help from our friends.' A few guys on the football team. Well, one of them, so far. Mike Clune. Maybe Will Martin." I hadn't actually asked Will.

"Seriously?" Josh said. "The Irishman'll stick his meat-neck out? For this?"

Simon flipped one of his sticks into the air. "Our own roadie!"

"Okay, so here's how it goes," I said. "We get there real early, get seats in the front row. That way, when Mario finishes and Clune brings the stuff on, we jump on the stage before anyone can stop us and just start playing."

"That'll be the first time I'll ever rush a stage because I

was supposed to be *on* it," said Simon. "One way or another, we are definitely going to go out on a good note."

"*Lots* of good notes," Josh said.

We were walking back to the dorms when I reached my hand out for Caroline's. She took it, eyes on the ground. Gentle squeeze. Just right. *Yes.*

"You really liked it?" I said.

"I loved it. It's beautiful and crazy and original. It breaks every rule of conventional music except the only one that counts: it reaches you." This girl was sort of amazing. "Unlike Hopper's robots, who play the Fifth like it's a math problem to solve." And then she twined her arm in mine. I mean, just come snatch me up. To heaven. Or wherevs. "Well, gotta get to sleep. Big meet." The last cross-country meet of the season was tomorrow. The whole league. "Will you be there?"

"I'll be there," I said. "How you guys going to do?"

"I don't know. Chelton and Essex supposedly have these super-fast runners."

"Its not just speed," I said, thinking of the Reservoir. "It's wanting it more than the next runner, right?"

"Well, I do know the course. I know those woods better than anyone. They're sort of enchanted by now. To me, anyway. See ya."

Enchanted.

· · ·

It was a sunny, cold, and crisp. A good day for a possible girlfriend to be running through her Dionysian woods. All I could think of during practice was Caroline running . . . with those long legs, in those shorts. After practice I hustled up the hill and into the showers so I could watch the end of the race.

A cluster of parents and coaches had gathered at the cross-country finish line, a few hundred yards away from the spot where the trail came out of the woods behind the football field—her woods. I moved away from the pack of parents to the spot where the trees gave way to the open field—just in time to see Caroline burst out of the woods, into the sun, in her Oakhurst blue tank top and those shorts and . . . wait . . . *first place?* With only one hundred yards left?

Then, about three seconds later, two girls, one from Chelton and one from Essex, came out into the clear, side by side, arms and legs pumping. They were gaining ground on her as the three sprinted across the grass toward the finish line.

She passed right by me, ponytail bouncing from side to side, snorting like a racehorse. She had this cool, steely, powerful look on her face, seeing nothing but the tape at the finish line. Then I saw her glance back to see where the others were, then look back at the tape—and just like that, the other two girls weren't closing in on her. Her back-kick was higher, her arms were pumping in perfect synch: she'd shifted into high gear. She was flying.

"Yeah, Callahan!" I shouted at her back, and started to run toward the finish line too. All I could see was Caroline shoving her arms straight up in the air.

She'd done it.

The crowd broke into polite applause. Most of them were visiting parents who'd figured their own daughters would win.

Then: one loud, joyous shout, a voice I knew very well. "YES!" Caroline was spinning in a circle, singing to the sky—and to the mountain behind her.

When I reached the finish line, Booth was high-fiving her. Caroline's return high five was less energetic than her stupid coach's. Then Caroline walked away, stopped, bent at the waist, hands on knees, exhausted. When she saw me, she rose up, laughed, and fell into my arms, half hugging, half hanging on to me for support. Damn, did she *still* ever smell good.

We broke apart.

"You're the star!" I said.

"I can't believe it," she said, gasping, her cheeks all pink, her eyes lit up. "I was behind them by about fifty feet until the course went into that trail in the woods for the last half mile, where you have to run on dirt and dodge the branches. They weren't used to running in a forest, I guess. I sort of had the home-field advantage."

"Yeah, well, give yourself a little credit, girl," I said. "*You* won the race. Not the trees. Where were your folks?"

"It's a weekday, stupid. They're both at work. They'll be here for the concert." Then she smiled a smile that had a whisper of some flirt to it. "Hey," she said. "Wait till I take a shower, then you want to go see that chimney on the mountain I told you about?"

"Yeah," I said. "I could do that." I could so do that.

Even after winning the race, she was amped enough to skip up through the woods, hopping from rock to rock, leaping over dead logs, while I kept falling behind. She'd stop and wait for me to catch up, smiling in a way I'd never seen her smile. She was on top of her world. And she was letting me into it.

It took a good half hour to get to the chimney. Sometimes we were jogging on dirt paths. Sometimes we were picking our way through big rocks in a dry stream. Sometimes we were going right through the forest, sweeping weeds and vines and dead branches and spiderwebs out of our faces.

Then we were at the top of the mountain I'd been looking up at all season, without ever seeing it like this: through its lens, as it had been watching us down below.

The stone chimney rose above an old blackened fireplace, and nothing else, in the middle of a small, windy clearing full of weeds. It was perched right on the edge of a little plot of land that looked down, like, a thousand feet below, on the school. It looked like a school in a model train set.

An outline in the stubbly grass around the chimney showed where the cabin had once stood, probably built by some guy whose signature was on the Constitution. The chimney was made of really old rocks.

"Isn't this cool?" she said. "It had to be someone's house, with gardens and everything. Someone's little farm."

We sat down, doing our usual shoulder-to-shoulder thing, our backs to the chimney. Way below, the shadow of the line of the setting sun was slowly crossing the athletic fields, edging up toward the campus. From here, you could see the quad and all the buildings around it, and how all the buildings of the old campus were laid out in a pattern. Once upon a very old time, Oakhurst Hall had some very old logic.

Then I felt her hand curl into mine, and all I hoped that mine didn't start sweating and short out the electricity.

The bell tower tolled five times. This time, each note sounded like music.

I felt her look over at me, only now there was a different look in her blue eyes. I'd never seen it, but I recognized it.

The kiss was a real kiss. She tasted warm, sweet, good. Just right.

When we pulled apart, neither of us said anything.

Now what? Was I supposed to make some heavy move? As usual, she took the lead.

She turned her face to the view below. "Look at the

campus," she said. "It's like a postcard, isn't it? Look at the way that shadow sort of crept over the whole school. It didn't even look like it was moving. Like nature moves. Slowly. But it gets where it's going."

"That's what Simon would say," I said, even though I wanted to move a little quicker.

Then she looked at me. She'd been reading my mind. "Jack," she said, "I like that pace. Slow."

And she stood up, and led me back down the hill. She was skipping. I was floating.

I HAD NEVER HEARD BACK FROM Dad. I didn't think he'd be here. But in a way, not knowing made me think I might play better. If he was out there, he'd be proud, and if he wasn't, then I was basically right about everything I thought about him. I'd still be playing for Caroline . . . and, yeah, for Oakhurst Hall. If I got to play much.

It was freezing. The sky was silver gray, and the air smelled like snow. Prepworld covered the hillside and flowed right down to the sideline, like those old pictures of baseball games from a hundred years ago where the fans would stand right up next to the field.

Over at one end, there was a cluster of men and women in fancy leather coats with fur collars and hats: Will's mom's family had come over from Spain. Brothers, sisters, uncles. They were smiling and laughing. And for the first time this year, I saw could see local people out there—*real* people: men wearing baseball caps, townie boys with buzz cuts and Engleside Eagles sweatshirts, and their girls, wearing parkas from mall outlets.

There were even a couple of fat guys in their thirties roaming the sideline with notebooks: sportswriters from

Concord and maybe even up from Worcester, because this game was news. A championship was on the line, even if it was a school that couldn't give a damn what the *Concord News-Times* thought. A title is a title.

And just like Madden had said, there were a couple of older guys, standing next to each other, wearing baseball caps from Ohio State and Michigan. He hadn't been bullshitting: Division I scouts.

Working out on the other sideline, the Essex guys looked big in their "evergreen and pewter" uniforms.

I scanned the hillside again and saw Ward's perfect little kids sticking their tongues out to collect the first snowflakes of the year, giggling, running around, and chasing the flakes like puppies, probably dreaming of sledding and skiing and whatever else little kids dream of before someone tells them they can't.

And then I saw Ward. He was walking toward me as I did leg lifts. With the clipboard. My stomach knotted. Okay. What the hell was *this* going to be about? He couldn't cut me. I didn't have any contraband in the room he could have found. He was not going to derail me. Not after almost three months of lifting. Three months of surviving. Three months of finding out who Jack Lefferts could be.

Just then, cheers started to spark up from the crowd: "Oak-hurst! Oak-hurst!" Then, from the grandstand on the visitors' side: "Es-sex! Es-sex!"

Now Ward stood over me. But he didn't look down. Just talked, fast. "We x-rayed Bannion's knee," he said. "Tore all the ligaments like they were string or something. Never seen one like that. Anyway, he's toast. You're starting. And we got no kicker." Then he walked away.

Oh, man. Oh, man. Starting. But I was ready. For the first time in my life, I felt like I was dealing from strength.

And I didn't have any more time to get nervous, because just then a different chant came up, sort of ragged, from a spot way down on the far end of the hill: "O-thers! O-thers!" I saw Josh and Danny and Simon. Sam and Seo Woon. And Caroline.

Turned out I was wrong when I told Clune that none of my family would be at the big game.

As the team gathered on the sideline, I ran in place to stay warm. The ground was hard, just a little forgiving. The earth was locking up, beginning the winter freeze. It would be tough to make sharp cuts on pass patterns with the plastic cleats. A slippery tabletop field would definitely favor the defenses. Runners would have trouble getting traction.

After we broke the pregame huddle, Madden walked over. Something about the captain looked different: he'd cut his golden locks off. His usual stony glare hinted at some nerves. This was his all-or-nothing moment.

"I'm going to go to you a lot today, if we can," said the quarterback. "Right?"

"Right," I said. "Totally."

"Okay, then," he said. "Let's beat these motherfuckers, and then I can leave this fun house behind." He snapped his chin strap like some guy flipping his Spartan helmet faceplate into place.

When it was finally time for me to lower my helmet over my head for the last time this season, I flashed back to the first day I'd put it on—how strange it had felt, how weird it was to see the world through that narrow slit.

This time, it felt comfortable, smelling of *my* sweat, as if I'd been wearing it for all the autumns of my life. This time, the view through the face mask wasn't foreign. It was a clear view on a world where I'd earned a place. Where, at least for the next few hours, I belonged.

A few yards away, Zowitzki and Thorn were butting each other like elk. Then Clune lumbered over and slammed his hands onto my shoulder pads like twin hammers. "You ready, man?"

I nodded. Week after week, I'd seen my teammates' faces enter into some kind of zone. Finally, I was there, too. I couldn't wait for the game to start.

Will came over—wearing the goofiest, most relaxed smile I'd ever seen. "I love the snow," he said. "I love playing in the snow. Good omen. The gods are with us."

"We won't need them." I said, trying to pump myself up.

"You always need them," Will said. "Big games always turn on something weird. Something fluky always happens that you never see coming."

. . .

Ward had been right about Essex's quarterback, Carson. The kid was a jackrabbit. After Mancini, enlisted into duty, kicked off by popping the ball more or less straight up in the air, on the first two plays, even with Zowitzki forcing him back to the inside, Carson scampered for first downs.

On the third play, Carson took the snap and, at the last second, pitched the ball outside to his running back. Everybody went for the running back, but before they could get there, he stopped and threw a pass to Carson, who had run downfield, unnoticed and untouched. Sixty yards later, it was 7–0, Essex.

"Check it out: the dude is wearing sneakers," Clune said to me on the sideline. He was right. Carson was wearing black sneakers with good treads while we were wearing old-fashioned cleats. The ground was getting harder and more slippery.

We came out nervous and flat. Anthony fumbled the kickoff and just managed to fall on the ball as the Essex kids piled onto him. Then Addison fumbled on his first carry, and Clune saved him by jumping on the loose ball. Madden overthrew Will on a square out, and the Essex linebacker, O'Doul, sacked Madden on third down.

Ward wanted to scream. But Bruno stood next to him with his hands folded, wearing a gray hoodie, the John Deere cap, and the expression of a guy watching corn grow. My guess was that the big man had told Ward that, in front of every alum and his wife, screaming wasn't the way to go.

When Essex got the ball back, Carson picked up where he'd left off, sprinting around the end, juking his way up the middle, eating up yardage. Essex was deep in Oakhurst territory when Carson turned the corner on a run. Thorn came up to try and tackle him, overran him on the slippery turf and reached back to clothesline him, ramming his forearm across the kid's throat.

Carson went flying, Thorn was called for a personal foul, and Essex had a first down on our five. Ward just shook his head, like it was Thorn's fault.

But this time we toughened up. Zowitzki forced Carson inside twice, where we stuffed him; he had no power once you stopped him. Then Mancini sacked him, bringing the full weight of his body to slam into Carson's ribs on the ground: an old-fashioned wrestling body slam.

The refs let it go. Mancini got up . . . and didn't pound his chest.

Now, on fourth down, Essex decided not to go for a field goal. Carson tried to sprint around the end and beat Zowitzki—but Thorn shoved him out of bounds—on the one-foot line.

We'd held. By twelve inches. The hillside went crazy.

"I don't know about you guys," Madden said in the huddle, "but I'm not gonna waste my shot at the Big Ten. We get it back—now. Ninety-nine yards. Start with Martin: down

and in and under the coverage. Their safeties are deep.
Line—give me time."

Madden led Will perfectly on a crossing route, twenty
yards downfield. As the receiver turned upfield, two Essex
kids hit him high and slammed him to the turf. His helmet
bounced on the ground.

"You okay, Will?" I asked in the huddle.

"Never better." He grinned. "Hey, you think the snow's
going to stick?"

"Martin," Madden said, "are you with us?"

Will winked at me. "I'm all here, Captain. Just get me
the ball. Today is our day. We've both been waiting four
years for this, right? Let's do it."

"Don't worry about Martin's head," said Clune. "He can
afford to lose a few brain cells."

The mood had changed. And then, with it, the momentum. Addison pounded out a first down with a couple of
runs, and Madden took advantage of Essex's all-out blitz to
tuck the ball in and slip up the middle for fifteen.

I ran a square in for five, catching the ball just as an
Essex defensive back speared me, helmet-to-helmet—a
retribution blow for Thorn's clothesline. For some reason,
though, he was the one who went down in a heap. Some
Essex guys helped him off the field. He had the thousand-
yard stare in his eyes: lights on, nobody home. Done for the
day.

I was fine. Maybe it was just physics: he hit me at the wrong angle.

I trotted back in just as Martin was calling a play for Madden. "Try that crossing route to me again, only, Jack, see if you can pick off that new DB who just replaced your other guy. He'll be scared shitless."

Madden led Martin perfectly, just as I crossed over to blindside the sub. I launched myself into midair, like some old-time football card. I'd look like an idiot if I missed the kid—but I didn't. I hit him square, he went flying, and Martin had acres of space. He sprinted the final thirty yards, untouched, for the tying touchdown.

The sound from the sideline was as sweet as symphonies get.

The snowfall was getting thicker. By the middle of the second quarter, both offenses began to stall, spinning their wheels. No one could get any footing on the field, because it was now nearly frozen. In the final minutes of the first half, Zowitzki cost us a touchdown: he sacked Carson, but yanked on the kid's face mask, twisting his head sideways. The flag flew: it'd be a fifteen-yarder.

As the linebacker rose, three Essex linemen surrounded him—and Zowitzki completely lost it. He went insane, shoving two of them, hard, then butting another with his helmet. A second flag flew. For once, I understood.

The referee marked off thirty yards.

"Goddammit," Ward said. But he didn't throw the clipboard or go nuts. He kept the kid in. It was a mistake. On the next play, Zowitzki blew into the backfield, out of control, trying to kill Carson—who calmly sidestepped him, took off down the field, and outran everyone for his second touchdown. It was 14–7, Essex, at the half.

As we gathered in the end zone for the final halftime huddle of the season, the snow was coming down steadily. The crowd was stamping its feet, hugging themselves to keep warm.

I didn't feel the cold. I just wanted the ball.

Bruno stood before us, eyes scanning the team, waiting patiently until he had everyone's attention. Then, in a quiet voice, the mysterious head coach began to speak.

"It's a funny thing," he said, "how life gives you second chances. There's the first act and the second act."

It was so silent I swear I could hear the flakes landing on my shoulder pads.

"Two more quarters," said the man. "Two quarters left until you meet your destiny. Use them more wisely than you did in the first half." He didn't look at Zowitzki. He didn't have to.

"We're doing all right," said Zowitzki. I think he'd overdosed on something. "If we can take out that fucking quarterback, we can win this game."

"Only a fool thinks winning has something to do with a score," Bruno said, as if he hadn't even heard Zowitzki. "Trust me. I've been there. I've coached teams that won a lot of football games. In a lot of ways. But there's only one right way: playing for the men on each side of you."

Now Bruno looked Zowitzki right in the eye. "This game is not about you. It's not about those people on that hillside. It's not about bringing glory to your school. It's not about your own personal glory. It's about the guy on each side of you. Doing right by him. Because he's the one who got you here."

He paused. I don't know about the rest of them, but he had me hooked. Then he started up again.

"Time was, I was blinded by the same light you're staring into, Mr. Zowitzki. But you have an advantage. You have a chance to step out of it. You have a chance to learn from the mistakes of the people who came before you. You have a chance to walk off this field as a winner. You all do."

Then Bruno turned to Ward. "Anything to add, Mr. Ward?"

The Clipboard Coach shook his head.

I pulled on my helmet. I was eager to get back into my personal cave. I ran in place for a few seconds and noticed the mountain looking down at me. Snow was starting to frost the branches, like powdered sugar. I trotted back to our bench and heard a voice behind—and slightly beneath—me.

"Hey, Jack?" Alex was standing in front of me with a

backpack. "Hey, listen, maybe one of these will fit," he said. "I just went from room to room in my dorm." And the little kid spilled a half dozen pairs of sneakers at my feet.

I grabbed a real fancy new pair with a good, thick, tread, and laced them on. Good enough. Actually, just about perfect.

"Maybe they won't slip as much," Alex said. I tossed him a football from the bag, ran a quick five yards, pivoted, felt the sneakers grab the hard turf. I took his pass in stride, then tossed the ball back to him.

"See you on the field next fall, right?" I said.

His bobblehead nodded. "Right!"

In the first huddle, Madden was calm. We were only down by one TD . . . but scoring was going to be hard in the snow. "Okay, let's get it back, quick. Jack, remember the flanker screen pass against Anglican? Do it again. Line up behind Martin, come back in toward me, and when you get it, just take off. Clune, you know what to do. Seal the lane. Will, pull that cornerback with you outside."

Madden took a quick drop, turned, and fired the ball to me. This time, I didn't bobble it. I cradled it and cut inside behind Clune's block on the linebacker as I crossed the line of scrimmage. Martin had lured the cornerback. Now I saw the safety take aim—until out of nowhere, Madden himself was there to tie the kid up.

I was heading for them full speed, so I cut upfield. The sneakers held.

Madden and the safety slipped to the ground.

I turned it on.

No one would catch me today.

As I sprinted toward the end zone, I heard nothing but the sound of my breath echoing in my helmet, as if someone had turned off the rest of the soundtrack.

Then I was in the end zone. Touchdown. And someone turned the soundtrack back on: I heard the hillside erupt, as background noise; the solo came from the girl whose face was almost completely hidden by her hooded gray sweatshirt, both fists thrust into the air. "Yeah, number eighty-eight!"

I acted like I'd been there before—tossing the ball to the ref before Martin gave me a bear hug. Back on the sideline, Bruno did a little fist-pump when I looked over at him. Anthony high-fived me . . . and Mancini, of all people, gave me a head-butt that nearly knocked me down.

It was a tie game, and by now, the snow was sticking. It seemed for sure that the next team to score would win, and things looked good when we took over on our own twenty-yard line with three minutes to play. But on the next play, Essex's linebacker O'Doul forced Addison to fumble, and Essex recovered the ball on our fifteen.

But the defense held. On third down, Mancini reached up and swatted down a pass. Essex lined up for a field goal from about thirty yards out: a tough kick through the swirling white confetti.

I watched from the sideline as the kick arced through the snow, came down—and, impossibly, bounced right onto the crossbar. Then it flipped straight into the air, came back down, hit the crossbar *again*—and rolled over the bar, into the end zone.

The ref's hands shot up: it was good.

It was the fluke that Martin had predicted. The unpredictable moment. The trick of the Football Fates—probably pissed off at Zowitzki.

Essex led 16–13, with just over two minutes left. We needed a touchdown to win.

Anthony shed two tackles and returned the Essex kickoff to the forty. The snow was driving. It was going to be hard to even see the ball on pass plays.

"Okay," Madden said in the huddle, his frozen breath puffing out in clouds, "here's the word—we pound it out. Can't risk the turnover. We try and run it down their throats. Right up the middle."

"Line!" barked Clune. "Let's blow 'em away!"

And for the next half dozen plays, Clune's boys did their jobs. We were down at the Essex twenty-five-yard line. But now Essex held. Two straight runs went nowhere.

"They know it's coming," Madden said in the huddle. "The run won't work anymore." He looked at me. "I'll hit you on a square out. They won't expect it."

Will turned to me. His voice had an extra edge. He was

hyped. I realized that the goofiness was partly an act; this really *did* mean everything to him. Dartmouth beckoned, then probably med school or politics. This might be the last kid moment of his life.

"You gotta bump the corner first," he told me. "Stay on your feet. Get him off you. Then run the pattern. So line— you *have* to hold the blocks, give Vic time."

We broke, and trotted out and lined up across from he Essex corner. The blankness in his eyes was spooky.

Now, it hit *me* how much this meant. The Reservoir, Outward Bound, the months of Ward's whining . . . I'd do more than bump the kid.

Madden barked the signals for what seemed like forever. Come on, *come on*! Then, finally, I broke at the snap, running as hard as I could, and met the kid head-on. Our helmets collided—clean, legal, and brutal, a stars-flashing blow, a millisecond of nothingness in my head.

Then everything came back into focus. The corner was still on his feet, but backing up, trying to get his footing. I broke to the outside, turned, and saw the ball coming at me. It was fast, it was high, and it was behind me—and a whole season of instinct took over as the ball whirled through the snow.

In my head, I was back on the quad on that first day, so long ago, gathering in the wild pass. I was back on the field for that first JV practice, catching everything that came my way. I was back in my first varsity practice, taking Zowitzki's hits. I was back in the touch games with Alex.

I leapt into the air, leaned back, and pulled the ball into my chest just as the cornerback slammed me out of bounds. I rolled on the hard turf, cradling the ball. I'd gained fifteen yards.

It was first down on their ten-yard line. Through the snow, I could see the lightbulbs of the scoreboard: 0:58. We had one time-out left.

Madden called Addison's number on runs, twice in a row, but they were keying on him, and with the slippery field, we couldn't move the pile. No yards.

On third down, Madden tried a pitchout wide to Anthony, who ducked under a kid's swipe but got shoved out of bounds on the six-yard line.

Madden called our last time-out with eleven seconds left. It had come down to one play. All or nothing.

I looked over to the Essex bench. The other team was screaming its lungs out. In the grandstand behind them, the visiting crowd was on its feet.

On the Oakhurst hillside, the cheers had blended into a single roar. In front of our bench, Ward was waving frantically with his clipboard for Madden to come over and get the play.

But Madden wasn't going anywhere. He turned his back on Ward and called us together for the final play of the season.

"Okay, Lefferts, the first pass I ever threw you is gonna be the same as the last pass I'll ever throw you: down and in.

Hold on to it. That O'Doul kid's gonna cream you. Pretend it's Zowitzki in that first practice. Piece of cake, right?"

Piece of cake. I knew I'd make the catch. Everything had been leading to this: one play, everything on the line. This play belonged to me.

Or did it?

All of a sudden, I knew what the real, unseen tip of fluky fate *had* to be.

"No," I said.

"*What?*" Madden said.

Ten sets of eyes fixed me in their stares.

"Martin," I said.

Madden couldn't believe it. "Lefferts, what the hell are you doing?"

"This one belongs to Will," I said. I turned to number eighty-five. "It's your last play here, and it wins a championship. You already told me this is your day, remember?"

Martin smiled at Madden. "You heard the man," Will said.

Madden stared at us both. Then he said, "Okay. What's it going to be?"

"That linebacker's gonna blitz you," he said. "So we have to do this quick. Jack and I flank wide, side by side, me to the outside. Jack breaks first, drifts to the sideline, draws the corner with him. I cross in behind him. The safety will be on me, but get it to me quick enough, high enough, it'll work."

Madden looked at Will. Then he looked at me. Then he nodded. "Martin on a slant, on one," said Madden. "Break."

Eleven pairs of hands clapped as one.

We broke the huddle. Will and I trotted to our positions. As Madden called the signals, Will and I looked at each other. We both nodded. This was it.

Madden took the snap. I broke to the outside, and the corner followed me, just like Will said he would. Will took off toward the middle behind me. I turned just in time to take it all in.

The Essex linebacker had broken through our line on a blitz, and he was twisting Madden down by his legs. But as he fell, Madden zipped the ball—fast, rising, a rope.

Will reached up and pulled it in.

The safety slammed into the big kid's thighs, flipping him. Will fell to the ground—and cradled the ball with both hands to his chest.

Touchdown. Championship.

I was the first one to reach him. We were engulfed, swarmed under a pile of limbs and bodies, rolling around as one, to the tune of the roar of the hillside. Sweet, sweet music.

As I untangled, I looked over at our sideline. Bruno's fist was thrust in the air. High. It stayed there. For everyone to see.

On the sideline, Ward was whooping, darting from player to player, pounding helmets, slapping butts.

Clune was hugging about a dozen different Dorchester homies.

Will's family—Guillermo's family—was dancing.

Zowitzki, with no one left to hit, was on his knees, pounding his helmet into the ground like a hammer, again and again, a kid possessed: "Yeah! Yeah!"

Thorn was lying a few yards away, doing nutsoid snow angels.

Madden was carrying Lucy over his shoulder, like a caveman with his woman, while she pounded his back with her fists, happy as hell.

Now Bruno was sitting on the bench. Alone. Leaning back with his arms spread, and smiling. I was anxious to get up onto the hillside. But I had to know. I sat down next to him and pulled off my helmet.

"Hell of a game, Jack," he said shaking my hand. "Congratulations. Next year that'll be you catching that pass."

"Congrats to you, Mr. Bruno. Hey, can I ask you something?"

He slowly turned to look at me, and I could see near-tears gathered in the crow's-feet at the corners of his eyes. Maybe this championship meant more to him than any of us. "Shoot."

"Did you know about the juicers?"

He looked back at the field and the celebrations, and nodded. "I had a feeling a few weeks in. Then, when we got Zowitzki's liver scan back, that more or less sealed it. But his numbers are low. He should be all right—as long as he gets off them. Which he will. And so will the others."

"But why didn't you stop it early on?"

He was silent, his expression calm. It was the look of a guy at peace with himself. I didn't want to ask the next question, the obvious one: Had he ignored it to win the title?

He'd read my mind. He looked back at the field. "Not so we'd win games, son. Trust me on that one. And don't think I didn't give it some real thought. But for one thing, I knew it was a handful of them, and that if I called them out on it, they wouldn't listen. Kids don't. They'll do the opposite of what we tell them. That's how you guys are wired.

"Plus, we didn't have any kind of real testing procedures in place. If I'd made Mancini piss in a cup, it'd have been two weeks at the earliest if we used a legit lab. Even then, the results could have been flawed. And there's stuff out there no one's got the tests for. More every year. On top of which, truth is, they may make you stronger, but they don't make you better. Bottom line?" He looked at me. "What is it they say in the Bible? 'He that is without sin among you, let him first cast a stone'?"

It took a second for that one to sink in. "You mean, you . . ."

He nodded. "You must've heard about my incident back in the day. Normal coaches don't slug their kids. Rage coaches do."

But he wasn't even a player. Coaches?

He read my mind again. "It was a big thing in D-III, back in the Alleghenies. Coal-country football. In our league, whoever could scream loudest and coached like a madman won the most games. That's how I used to coach. With a little help from the same stuff my players took."

It was almost all too much to take in. "But then shouldn't you have warned—"

"Wasn't my place," he said. "Education isn't about lectures or threats. It's about teaching how to learn. They'll learn when they're ready. Not before. Zowitzi wasn't ready to learn. Me, I learned a lot of things. Like when to turn it on, and when to let it be. You're learning. I think you know that. And don't worry. Next year's team won't have any Zowitzkis—even if Williamton and Essex will be just as juiced as always. Now, get out of here. Your friends are waiting for you."

He slapped my thigh-pad. I stood up. "And one more thing, Jack. Zowitzki and Addison and Thorn and Mancini didn't win this trophy. You and Anthony and Will and Clune did. Have a nice Thanksgiving. See you in class."

And then, up on the hillside, I was surrounded.

"Nice game, number eighty-eight," said Caroline. "You're a star." I had to fight back the impulse to kiss her.

Seo Woon ruffled my hair. Josh said, "Pretty cool, dude. But they shoulda thrown you that last pass."

Sam said, "That was exciting. Who won?"

• • •

There was bedlam in the locker room—shouts echoing out of the showers, kids tossing equipment at one another. I sat in front of my locker, still in full uniform, letting the joy soak in.

"That was a big-time move, Lefferts," said Clune, holding out a meaty paw. "Couldn't believe it when you said it. That's gotta be a first-timer for old Oak."

"Not bad for a couple of JVs!" Garver shouted, high-fiving me. "Can you believe this?"

"Yeah," I said. "I can believe it. I can definitely believe it."

Will drifted over and offered me a firm handshake. "I owe you, little man. Big time. You *know* you're looking at being captain next year, right?"

Next year? "I just figured we had a better chance throwing the ball to our best receiver," I said. "Someone who'd been there before."

"Well," he said, "now it's your turn. Tonight's the *real* pressure, right? Clune told me what to do." He grinned. "Look out, Oak-land."

"You sure you want to do this?" I said. "We're all gonna catch some major shit."

"We've got your back," Martin said. "No worries. I wouldn't miss it for the world. You just better play your asses off."

THE AUCHINCLOSS CONCERT AUDITORIUM HAD ABOUT fifty rows of dark-blue-velvet-upholstered seats, opera-style boxes up in the wings, and another couple dozen rows of gold-velvet-upholstered seats up in the balcony. Huge acoustic baffles loomed behind the stage. Six rows of stage lights stared down. And somewhere up there was a chandelier shaped like—I swear—a lion's head.

We got there a half hour before the concert to stake out a front-row perch—only to discover that gold-velvet ropes on the aisles were blocking off the first twenty rows: RESERVED FOR FACULTY, ADMINISTRATION, AND PARENTS OF THE MUSICIANS read the signs hanging from the ropes. Programs in blue leather binders had been carefully placed on each of the roped-off seats.

"Okay, so we can't hop onstage as quick—no big deal," I said as coolly as I could, as we took four seats on the aisle—twenty-one rows back.

"We're fucked," Josh said. "We'll never get up there in time."

"We'll just have to hustle a little more," Danny said.

"Jack, you sure your guys are in on this?" Simon said.

"They'll be there. They'll have our backs." I believed it.
I really did.

I grabbed a leather program and read the evening's agenda:
After the symphony played the Fifth, Mario Miles would, in-
deed, be playing selections from Rachmaninoff's Third
Piano Concerto. He was going to go for it all.

The Thanksgiving concert was obviously High Ritual. The
faculty started to file in wearing suits and dresses. Parents were
dressed to the hilt. Perfume, cologne, the jingle of jewelry. I
tried to cool out, to remember Jarvis: Let go, or be dragged.

In the front row, Carlton wore a tuxedo, sitting next to
guys who had to be honcho board members: suits, school
ties. Booth and Ward were working their way up and down
the aisles, taking attendance. Mandatory attendance had
been announced that week.

"The famous band!" said Ward, in a buoyant mood, as
he checked off our names. "You're in for some *real* music,
gentlemen. Enjoy the concert."

"I'm sure we will, sir," said Josh. "We're very excited. But
hey, what's with the attendance thing? I mean, the term's
technically over, right?"

"TV." He pointed to a camera crew up in one of the
opera boxes. "WGBH, Boston. We don't want empty seats,
do we?"

. . .

Exactly at seven P.M., the symphony entered, to loud applause. Sam carried his cello, Seo Woon her viola. And
then I saw the third-seat flute: hair pulled back in a ponytail, wearing a sleeveless black gown and a single strand of
pearls . . . Man, did she look great.

Hopper came out from the wings to mild applause,
wearing white tie and tails. "I can't thank you all enough for
coming and helping Oakhurst Hall support the arts," the
maestro said, cheerily. "You're in for a very special evening.
As you all know, in the past, our brilliant young musicians
have put on many truly remarkable performances. But tonight, I think, promises to be a truly memorable event."

"You got that right," said Simon.

The lights went down. Hopper turned and raised his
baton, Beethoven's most famous four notes exploded into
the hall, and for the next forty minutes, the Oakhurst Symphony, I had to admit, *was* spectacular. It didn't sound like it
was going through the motions to me.

By the third movement, I was too nervous to pay much
attention. Part of me worried whether we could make it onto
the stage when Mario finished, without the faculty—well,
Ward and Booth—heading us off. Those aisles were pretty
thin.

But mostly I was suddenly wondering whether our own
song was even half as good as I thought it was. More than

wondering. Kind of panicking. I'd been so freaked about pulling this thing off, I hadn't really stopped to wonder whether we were kidding ourselves. I mean, except for Jill McGregor everyone who liked it was a friend. What if we sucked? What if we'd just Krazy-Glued pieces of three hundred years of music into a quarter hour of randomness and we were going to make total fools of ourselves? Was I mistaking all the encouragement for politeness?

And what would the consequences be? *What if I do really leave this place, like, tonight? Where else am I going to grow up?*

No. Unh-unh. We might not be the Who, but we didn't suck. If I was wrong about that, then I was wrong about everything.

When the Fifth was finished, with its amazing final flourish, the musicians stood and bowed, to a standing ovation. Then they filed off, carrying their music stands, as the maintenance crew—in collared shirts and khakis—took the folding chairs into the wings and gently wheeled a Steinway grand onto center stage. The one Hopper had mentioned that first day. 1859. Maple filigree and gold-embossed lettering.

The auditorium silenced in anticipation.

Mario walked onto the stage, and I had to laugh: his tuxedo was about three sizes too small, and his bowtie was off-center. Plus, he was blushing like a ripe tomato. At least he hadn't worn an anarchy-symbol T-shirt. As applause rippled through the room, he gave an awkward bow, sat down, lowered his hands to the keys, and began to play . . .

. . . Gershwin's Three Preludes for Piano.

Maybe it was like an appetizer, I thought. A little warm-up to sneak in before the real fireworks. For fun.

For the next few minutes—nine to be exact, the total length of the preludes—I stopped worrying, blown away .by Mario's amazing gift. This was as beautifully as I'd ever heard anyone play the piano.

When he finished the last allegro, he tucked his hands back into his lap and lowered his head. I waited for those first, ominous, heavy Rach 3 notes.

But instead, Mario stood up and reached for the microphone that had been hovering over the piano's strings.

"Thank you," he said. "Thank you to Mr. Hopper, and to Oakhurst Hall for all its support of this great music program. Now, please enjoy the rest of the show. The fun has just begun."

And he walked off the stage. The crowd began to murmur: in front, worried. In back, excited.

What about the Rach?

There was no Rach.

The next thing I saw was Martin coming out of the right wings carrying Simon's bass drum and cymbal, followed by Clune coming out of the left wings with a snare and a tom-tom . . . and Mario now coming back out onto the stage—

carrying two amps and a bunch of cords, followed by Alex, who frantically started plugging them all in.

"Come on, let's GO!" Josh said, pushing me. The rest of the band piled into the aisle and walked quickly down the carpet. I was last. Out of the corner of my eye, I spotted Carlton and Ward down in the front row, talking like madmen.

I glanced up at the stage. Clune and Martin were carrying Josh's guitar and Danny's bass, and Alex and Mario were tapping the mikes.

The rest of the band was already on the stage when I heard Carlton's angry voice behind me: "Jack! What is going on here?"

I turned to see Ward in my face. "Lefferts, you have gone *way* over the line!"

I looked back at Carlton. He had turned around to look at the crowd. I think he wanted to shout out some sort of speech. A few faculty were on their feet, but the parents and their jewelry were still in their seats. Meanwhile, all the kids seemed to be cheering and clapping.

Now the head's eyes met mine. He was caught. For once, the man in charge didn't know what to do. This one was something he hadn't seen coming.

I grabbed the lip of the stage, vaulted myself up, and walked quickly to the sacred Steinway.

Mario had poised the mike above the piano wires: one

piano man looking out for another. I stared at the keys. All eighty-eight of them.

The crowd was quieting. Somehow, we'd made it to the stage. And somewhere I had the feeling that, right now, it was *our* school now.

I saw Carlton sit down. His eyes were closed. He was probably praying.

I looked around at the band and then I saw three extra chairs, with three extra microphones in front of them. And now, from the wings, Sam walked onto the stage with his cello, Seo Woon with her viola—and Caroline, fingering her flute, gracefully lowering herself into her seat, in her cool, long black dress, adjusting her microphone.

Then she was smiling over at me.

The huge auditorium was now completely silent. Not a squeak. Not a breath. Time was frozen, waiting for me.

"Go *ahead*," Caroline whispered, loud enough for everyone onstage to hear. "It's okay, Jack. You've done it. You've won. So *play*, you idiot," she said.

I took a deep breath, looked around at the band—the ensemble!—and gave a nod. The next thing I heard was Josh's guitar: the lively notes of a bird at dawn . . . only this time, each note was doubled by Caroline's flute.

My fingers played the Schubert notes, on their own . . . and I heard Sam and Seo Woon's strings backing me, harmonizing, the two of them watching me lead.

Now Simon snared the drum . . . and Danny's bass notes began to rise . . . and we played. No. This time, the song not only seemed to be playing itself, it seemed to be swelling, sounding even bigger, sweeter, grander in this acoustic-perfect cathedral—which, despite all the gilt, suddenly seemed to be a *room*.

I allowed myself a glance down at the crowd, too nervous to focus, but I could tell, as my eyes and brain took in everything at hyperspeed, as the notes unfolded on their own, and my fingers played, free of my brain, that hundreds of faces were smiling. Heads were nodding.

They liked it.

We shifted into the second movement, when the music began to rock—and with it, so did the students. In the back rows, kids were standing up and swaying and dancing to the sound of Simon's driving drums, Danny's hard, angry bass. Josh's guitar notes soared, climbing, angrily, deliriously.

Off to my left, Seo Woon's hair was flying from side to side as she played her rock viola. Sam was sawing at the strings of his cello. Caroline, flute on lap, was nodding and waiting for the next piece of quiet. And smiling.

And then we moved into the final movement, drifting toward the calm. The simple, clean melody took us home, to one last surprise: Caroline's flute, in the final measures, echoing the birdsong from the beginning . . . and closing it up like a sort of, well, symphony. With her final, drifting, plaintive notes, it was over. The echo of the flute receded into the last recesses of the hall.

Silence. Not a sound from the auditorium.

I glanced around the stage. My friends were all looking back at me, with expressions of delight and bewilderment, glee and triumph.

Did that just really happen?

And now what?

I knew what.

I stuck a fist high into the air—Bruno style—and I was only dimly aware of the eruption of applause in front of me, of the audience rising to its feet, in waves.

And of Jill McGregor shouting "Bravo!" from the second row.

And of Carlton, just below me, expressionless, like he'd been steamrollered.

And of angry Ward, seeing blood.

And of the band high-fiving and whooping all around me.

And then, of Caroline throwing her arms around me.

"You did it," she said into my ear.

"I love you," I said.

She didn't answer. Moving slowly. "See you next week, right?"

"That's up to the powers."

"I have a feeling you pulled it off. Okay, gotta run. Long drive back."

With that, she hopped off the stage. I walked to the edge to watch her dash up the aisle. Then a guy in a black suit and a white T-shirt came up to the stage.

"Nice stuff, guys. I'm Jim Trabucco. Sony." He was holding a card up in the air. Josh and I looked at each other.

Josh leaned down to take the card. "You liked it?"

"Don't get too excited. I'm with the classics side. But nobody told me about you guys. I'd like to hear more sometime." And with that, he was gone.

"Yes!" said Danny.

"Yeah," said Simon. "Except we don't have any more songs."

"No worries," said Danny. "It was great. *We* were great. And no matter what happens next," he said, nodding at Ward, who was now standing ominously beneath us, arms crossed, "this is a day dear old Oakhurst Hall's's never going to forget."

Then, one by one, we dropped down to the floor. To face the music.

"This is serious shit, assholes," Ward said, trying to keep his composure. Behind him, I saw a half dozen parents congratulating the headmaster, smiling, shaking his hand, just vaguely aware of Ward's voice:

". . . defying the headmaster's order not to play your song . . . disrupting . . . grandest traditions . . . taking the spotlight off those who deserved it . . . you will be hearing from me during vacation. I will be contacting all of your parents. And during that time, I want to you to consider the gravity of what you have done."

He stalked away.

We stood in silence. Then Josh laughed. "It was *so* worth it, whatever happens."

Now Carlton was at my side. "Young man, let's step outside for a moment."

I led the way, pushing open the emergency-exit door. I hoped I was ready for this.

It had stopped snowing. I steeled myself for the lecture.

"Like a postcard, isn't it?" Carlton said.

What?

It was true, though: half a foot of white stuff frosted the ground around us, and the bushes, and the perfectly hewn trees, like a blanket with little diamond-winks in it.

The lights through the auditorium windows cast slanted yellow rectangles onto the snow.

"Jack," he said, "you have put me in a very difficult position."

I tried to keep my mouth shut. I really did. But he seemed so quiet, almost normal, that I figured I might as well take my shot. "Maybe, sir," I said, "you helped put yourself there."

I waited for the eruption. Instead came the silence of the snowscape. Then he spoke quietly. "It's not as if I haven't tried to encourage the students to think outside the box," he said, sort of to me, and sort of to himself.

"Oakhurst Hall *is* a box, sir," I said. "But the rest of the world isn't boxed in anymore. There aren't any boxes. There are clouds. And I know that you think you have to follow some unwritten set of rules about how if we teach kids to get rich, they'll give money back to dear old—"

"It's not unwritten, Jack," he interrupted, but that was okay, because I could tell that for once, we were on an even playing field. "It's called 'the Board.' Speaking of which, two members have already congratulated me about your . . . performance. One of them even thought the whole thing was my idea." He smiled a real smile. "I believe Willis Thorn's words were, 'Glad to see you're ushering the place into the twenty-first century.' Pompous ass, that man. But he did suggest that he'd be the point man on fund-raising for a new arts building."

"Like, *all* the arts, sir?" I said. "Like making paintings with a phone app? Like taping oral histories? Like learning how to draw graphic novels?"

"Jack, be serious. There have to be boundaries."

"Well, yeah, sure. We're not against rules. But the thing is . . . you have to trust us. Come on, how many kids here actually dream about getting a Christmas bonus from First Boston—not because their parents want them to, but *they* want to?"

He had no answer.

Then he bent down, made a snowball, and whipped it into the darkness. It splatted perfectly against the middle of a tree trunk. Carlton *had* been a quarterback.

"Does this mean I can come back?" I said.

"You want to?" he said.

"If things can change."

He sort of smiled. "Jack, remember when you asked me if I was listening? If I heard it? The music?"

"Yes sir."

"I heard it tonight, son. Happy Thanksgiving." His handshake was cold. "Look forward to seeing you in a week." He put his hand on the doorknob, then stopped. "You don't happen to play basketball, do you, Jack?"

"No, sir," I said. "In the winter, my sport is sledding."

I walked over to the window and looked inside. Kids were milling around, enjoying the vibe. Madden was actually helping Clune and Martin lug equipment offstage. They had it under control. And Josh had somehow corralled the Sony guy. No doubt telling him about the other songs we hadn't even thought of yet.

And, of course, Tom and Ginny were talking with Ms. Booth, frowning about the end of twenty-first-century civilization.

I turned around and walked a few yards through the

snow, facing the mountain. Maybe that's why I wanted to come back to this stupid place: the mountain. I really liked that mountain.

It began to snow again: whirls of perfect, white flakes.

I heard the door open and turned around. At first, I didn't recognize him in the half dark. He was dressed in some full-length cashmere coat, and his hair had been gelled perfectly, and the suit had to have cost five grand. But the broken nose of the old hockey player gave him away.

"You made it," I said.

"I made it," Dad said. "All the Cayennes were booked."

"Did you see it all? The concert? The game?"

"Every minute," he said. "Those were some tough hits you took."

"But why didn't you tell me you were here?"

Because today was *your* day. Come on, let's get out of here. I'm freezing."

We tromped up the path to the parking lot, and as he shook snow off his wing tips, Dad hit the key to unlock the Lexus.

I piled into the passenger seat, and he turned the heat on. The seat smelled like Grace's perfume. This time, it didn't bother me. I kind of even liked it.

"You have to go by the dorm, get stuff?" he said. "Sign out?"

I probably should have. But for right now, I was done with the rules.

"Nah," I said. "It's not like I won't be back pretty soon. Let's go."

"Good," he said. "Let's bop down to Boston. I got us a suite at the Eliot. Four stars. You can wear those clothes till tomorrow."

We rode down the winding drive. Covered in snow, that weird sculpture looked almost pretty.

"That was a hell of a catch, at the end there, setting up the winning score," he said. "A *hell* of a catch. But why didn't they throw it to you for the winner?"

"Maybe next year," I said.

"Too bad you're so small. Otherwise—"

I interrupted him. "Otherwise I could go on to play college football? Use it to network . . . *for the rest of my life?*"

He laughed. "Something like that."

"That's then, Dad. That's the future. This is now. Like you said: This is my time. I'm going to enjoy it. Let me have it, okay?"

He looked over, his face bathed by the blue dashboard lights. He nodded.

We were about to pass Jarvis's house. His study light was on. I asked Dad to pull over, then knocked on the door. Jarvis was there in a dress shirt open to a T-shirt, with a cigarette in his mouth.

"Hey," he said. "Nice game. Nice song too. Well played, sir. Well played. Come on in."

"Naw, my dad's waiting out there. But I was wondering if you'd do me a favor."

"Sure."

A few minutes later, we were back on the road toward Boston. I was thumbing through the latest V. R. Hamilton epic by the light of the radio—the book autographed to Luke. He was going to flip.